CLONING ELVIS

ALSO BY BRIAN DAVID FLOYD

Livin' on a Prayer (with Robert Slawsby)
Last Wishes
Dad Was Right: 10 Life Lessons a Father Taught His Son
The Short Stack: Four Short Stories and One Random Poem

Learn more about Brian and get free stories at
BrianDavidFloyd.com

CLONING ELVIS

BRIAN DAVID FLOYD

This is a work of fiction. Names, characters, places, and incidents either are the product of the author's imagination or are used fictitiously.

Although Elvis Presley is a historical figure, nothing written here about him or anyone else should be taken as factual.

Elvis Presley Enterprises, Inc. does not substantiate, validate, or otherwise endorse the content of this book.

Print Edition

Cover design by Rocío Martín Osuna
DNA Chains used in the cover design and interior created by Freepik

First Edition
ISBN: 978-0-692-07447-3

For Mike

Thanks for sharing your infectious excitement for Elvis and the joy one experiences by channeling the King. Thank you. Thank you very much.

"Before Elvis there was nothing."

John Lennon

ELVIS WASN'T DEAD.

At least, he didn't think he was.

He opened his eyes with great effort. He always had a rough time waking up. There wasn't anything unusual about that. But the bright white light hanging over his face forcing him to squint was out of place.

Elvis sat up in the narrow bed his overweight body occupied and looked around. He was in a white room with only two straight-backed chairs and a table as furniture. He glanced down to find his body covered only by a sheet.

Where the heck was he? Was this a hospital? Had he gotten sick on tour?

"Good morning, Mr. Presley," a woman said. He hadn't noticed anyone else in the room.

Elvis turned his head to the left. A pretty woman wearing a white lab coat came toward him. She looked a lot like Priscilla, but it wasn't her. Behind her stood a smiling man with a hairline that had long ago retreated to the top of his head.

"How are you feeling?" she asked.

"Like I got hit head-on by a Mack truck," Elvis said. His head hurt, and he laid it back down on the pillow. "What happened to me? Where the heck am I?"

"That's a bit of the story," she said. "Perhaps the best place for us to start is if you'll tell me what the last thing you remember was."

"Uh, yeah," Elvis said. He took a few seconds to run through his memories. "I'd just finished my show in Springfield."

PART I

MOODY BLUE

CHAPTER 1

June 17, 1977
Springfield, Missouri

ELVIS WASN'T DEAD.

But he would be soon. He knew it.

That was what went through his mind as he sang "It's Now or Never" to the audience packed into the Hammons Center of Southwest Missouri University that Friday night.

He hated to admit it, but his life was in shambles. His existence had become a miserable routine of nonstop touring. Since Priscilla divorced him, he hadn't had a fulfilling relationship. They'd all been superficial and shallow.

Maybe those words best fit him too.

Despite all he'd achieved, all of the dreams of his youth that had come true, the words *superficial* and *shallow* seemed the best to describe his life. For a man who had nearly everything, feelings of loneliness and despair seldom departed from him.

Yet his adoring fans didn't seem to notice. They still loved him even as his rhinestone-studded jumpsuit bulged in his midsection. They didn't seem to notice how out of shape and overweight he'd become. Either that or they didn't care. He tried to ignore his immense size too, but the mirror didn't lie to him. It never had.

"Thank you, thank you very much, ladies and gentlemen," Elvis said as the song came to a close. He wiped the sweat from his forehead with a scarf and went to the edge of the stage. He bent down and handed it to a smiling woman in the front row. Charlie Hodge came out and placed a fresh scarf around his thick neck.

Elvis took a few seconds to catch his breath. He looked out upon the vast crowd filling the auditorium to capacity. Yep, they still loved him. They packed every place he performed. The women still screamed wildly like they had when they were teenage girls. They still couldn't take their mesmerized eyes off him. It had been their obsession with him that had skyrocketed him up to the stratosphere of fame. It had also built the solitary prison he'd been forced to live in for a bit more than twenty years now.

Yet he knew he'd be nothing without them.

Elvis smiled and snapped himself out of the introspection.

"You've really been a wonderful audience tonight. Now I'd like to leave you with a song from *Blue Hawaii.* If we never meet again, may God bless you and a-dios."

On cue, his Taking Care of Business band began one of the favorite songs he had ever recorded from one of his more tolerable movies, "Can't Help Falling in Love."

Elvis looked out at the crowd again. In one way or another, they were the ones responsible for everything that had happened. Would they have noticed if he'd never recorded a single song?

Of course not.

Would any of them even miss him when he was gone?

He doubted they would.

CHAPTER 2

BY THE TIME AL DVORIN announced, "Elvis has left the building," Elvis and his entourage, the so-called Memphis Mafia, were in their convoy of limousines headed back to the hotel.

Elvis had always hated the name Memphis Mafia. It made his entourage sound like criminals and leg-breakers. They were his friends. Some even family. Yes, he paid them, but who else could he really trust?

Maybe he couldn't trust any of them. After how Red, Sonny, and Dave had backstabbed him writing that damned trashy book, he wasn't sure who was really on his side. They'd all sell him out and splash his secrets everywhere for the right price. Wouldn't they?

The three limos pulled up to the rear entrance of the hotel. The hotel's manager waited for them there. He escorted Elvis and the fellas inside to a waiting elevator, up to the top floor, and into the hotel's largest suite.

Things got off to a bad start when Elvis saw his dinner wasn't waiting for him there, as he always expected it to be.

"Where the heck's the room service?" Elvis asked of no one in particular.

"It should be here," Joe said. "I'll check on it."

Joe Esposito picked up a phone on the table. Joe was Elvis's road manager, but also one of his closest friends. They'd met when the Army had stationed them both in

Germany. Elvis had hit it off with Joe and Charlie Hodge when the three were serving there, even though Elvis had known Charlie from well before getting drafted. The three had remained friends all of these years. Joe knew him better than anyone, and Elvis believed he really could trust him.

"And what about the cinema?" Elvis asked. "I really wanna get out and see a movie tonight."

"Their last show lets out at eleven," Elvis's stepbrother David said. "After that, the theater's all yours."

"They got that *Star Wars* picture playing?" Elvis asked.

"Sorry, E, not yet. But they do got *Smokey and the Bandit*."

"Dammit. Can't they get anything right here in Missouri?"

Elvis grabbed the ashtray from the coffee table and hurled it across the room. Lamar Fike and Charlie Hodge jumped out of the way to dodge it. The ashtray hit the wall behind them, but didn't break. But the impact did leave a good dent. As usual, the hotel would bill Elvis for the damage.

The suite's doorbell rang. David opened it and a bellboy pulled through two wheeled carts carrying the group's luggage.

"Well, at least the suitcases found their way up here," Elvis said. "Where the heck's my damn dinner?"

"Right here, Mr. Presley," a woman softly said from the doorway.

An attractive woman in her early twenties with her hair up pushed a cart of covered food into the suite. Elvis was about to give her a piece of his mind when he noticed she was in the last months of a pregnancy.

"I'm sorry for the delay, Mr. Presley," she said as she wheeled in the cart. "I noticed the mashed potatoes were cold and I had them cook you up some new ones."

"Well, that's mighty thoughtful of you," Elvis said, his

temper already lowered. "But my name's Elvis. Call me Elvis. You look like you should be home resting, not slaving away here."

"Oh, I'm fine, Mr. Presley…I mean, Elvis," she said. "I'm still a couple of months from my due date, and this work isn't too hard."

Elvis noticed the bellboy had finished offloading the luggage. He motioned to Lamar, who brought him his wallet. Elvis pulled a hundred-dollar bill from it and handed it to the bellboy.

"Thanks for bringing the bags up," Elvis said.

"You're welcome," the bellboy said. "If there's anything else you need, please let me know."

"We're going out to catch a movie in a little while," Joe said. "If you could come in and turn down the room and bring some extra towels, we'd appreciate it."

"I certainly will," the bellboy said, then hustled out of the suite.

Elvis returned his attention to the pregnant woman removing stainless steel lids from his dinner.

"That all looks and smells delicious," he said.

"I hope it is. If you need anything else, please let me know."

"Actually, you're the one who should be letting me know if there's anything else I can do for you."

"Oh, I'm fine, Mr. Presley."

"Elvis," he reminded her.

"Yes, I really don't need anything, Elvis."

"That may be, but is there anything you might want?"

She blushed a little and looked away from him.

"I'm not supposed to bother our guests, especially ones like you. But if there was any way I could get your autograph, it would mean the world to me."

Lamar was already handing Elvis a pad of paper and a

pen.

"And what's your name, little lady?" Elvis asked.

"Jennie. But I spell it with an IE, not a Y."

Elvis scribbled her name on the paper then his own. He ripped the page from the pad and handed it to Jennie.

"Thanks for bringing up my supper," he said.

"I hope everything tastes good."

"I'm sure it will. But wait a minute here. You can't leave without me tipping you."

Elvis pulled a wad of hundred-dollar bills from his wallet, peeled off ten, and handed them to her.

Jennie gasped. "Oh, Mr. Presley…I can't accept this much."

Elvis had seen both genuine and fake modesty from countless people over the years when he had given gifts. He always felt great when he encountered the real thing, like he was now with Jennie.

Elvis took her hand in his and put the cash in her palm. With his other hand, he closed her fingers around the thousand dollars.

"Consider it a gift for your baby," he said.

Jennie struggled to find words, then spoke after a few seconds. "I really don't know what to say."

"Ain't nothing to say. Thanks again for bringing up my supper."

"Thank you! Thank you, Elvis!"

Jennie threw her arms around him, giving him a big hug. Elvis smiled and led her to the door.

"You're very welcome, Jennie who spells it with an IE and not a Y."

Joe opened the suite's double doors to let Jennie out. She backed out of the room, smiling with pure happiness and joy. Elvis had made her night. And she had made his.

As Joe shut the doors, Elvis turned his attention to the

food before him. He plunged a fork into the mashed potatoes, collected a big scoop, and shoved it into his mouth. They weren't as good as the ones Mama used to make. Nobody's were, even though Dodger's came close. But these were good.

"Ain't Jerry Reed in *Smokey and the Bandit?*" Elvis asked whoever might answer.

It was Joe who did. "Yeah. So are Burt Reynolds and Jackie Gleason."

Good old Jackie Gleason. He'd hosted Elvis on his first television appearance in '56 with the Dorsey Brothers. After the show, Jackie had advised Elvis to never stop going out in the public. He'd warned Elvis that he'd be building himself a prison and would be the loneliest guy on the planet.

Elvis knew he should have listened. The thought started to depress him, and he shook it off.

"If it's got all them in it, it's gotta be a good picture," Elvis said. "We'll see *Star Wars* when Lisa Marie comes to visit me."

Elvis moved into the master bedroom to take off the damp jumpsuit and change into something more comfortable for the rest of the night.

CHAPTER 3

JENNIE CALLED HER HUSBAND FROM one of the four pay phones in the hotel's lobby to tell him about the thousand-dollar tip from Elvis. The money would go a long way in easing their financial pressures as a child was added to their family. Tears of joy fell from her eyes as she told him of their good fortune and Elvis's amazing generosity.

After hanging up with him, Jennie shared the story with everyone else also working the night shift. All of her coworkers were excited for her. They all considered Jennie one of the kindest and hardest-working people they knew. If anyone deserved such a generous tip, it was Jennie. They were all genuinely happy for the expectant mother.

All except one, a bellboy named Randall Briggs.

Her story pissed him off like nothing else.

Elvis had only handed Randall a single hundred-dollar bill for all the baggage he'd hauled up to the suite.

A one-hundred-dollar tip was the biggest Randall had ever received as a bellboy. At the time, he couldn't believe Elvis had given him that much. But then he heard Jennie talking about the thousand dollars he'd handed her for simply brining up some food. She'd probably played up her pregnancy to get the extra cash.

Randall had put in more work than she had. He deserved at least the same amount as a tip. And if Elvis wasn't handing it out, then Randall would find another way to get it.

Thirty minutes later, Randall made his move.

After Elvis and his hanger-on-ers had left for the movies, Randall headed back up to the suite as he'd promised. He first turned down the king-size bed and put clean towels in the large bathroom. Then he rummaged through Elvis's luggage. He searched through the pockets of all his clothes. He opened and closed every drawer, yet was careful to ensure that nothing appeared disturbed.

Randall found a shaving kit containing packets of pills in the bathroom. He wasn't sure exactly what they were, but he suspected they were illegal. All of the singers these days were stoned all the time. Jimi Hendrix, Janis Joplin, and Jim Morrison had all ODed and died.

Maybe this stingy lard-ass Elvis would suffer the same fate.

Good. The cheapskate deserved it, Randall thought as he continued his search for cash.

But there wasn't any money for him to find. Elvis may have been rich and handed out hundred-dollar bills like they were licorice, but he didn't leave his bankroll lying around. Coming up empty-handed infuriated Randall even more. One way or the other, he was going to get what Elvis rightfully owed him.

He thought of taking the drugs. He could probably find some people to sell them to, but he wasn't sure what the pills were. He also didn't have the first clue about finding out what they were and what they did. There had to be something else here he could take and sell for a nice little profit.

Randall went back into the walk-in closet. Before him hung the sweaty rhinestone-studded white jumpsuit Elvis had worn into the hotel from his earlier concert. Now that thing had to be worth at least a thousand dollars. No, it would go for more than that to one of Elvis's stupid, obsessed fans.

Randall pulled the jumpsuit from its hanger, folded it up as small as possible, and sandwiched it between the dirty towels. He picked the bundle up and stood in front of the wall-length mirror. No one would be able to tell he carried anything but a mass of soiled towels headed for the laundry. Randall smiled at his cleverness.

How he would make money from it, he wasn't exactly sure, but he knew someone somewhere would pay top dollar for a gaudy jumpsuit that had been worn by the so-called King of Rock and Roll.

CHAPTER 4

Tuesday, August 16, 1977

JENNIE HAD BEGUN MATERNITY LEAVE from the hotel the day before. Although she looked like she'd swallowed a medicine ball and felt as large as a houseboat, she had no clue when she might go into labor.

Rather than sitting around the house and simply waiting, Jennie used her unknown amount of free time to get the baby's room ready in the two-bedroom house she and her husband were renting. They had no idea if the baby was going to be a boy or a girl. Everyone thought it would be a girl, but Jennie had a suspicion she'd be having a boy.

As Jennie put the mattress into the baby crib she'd been given from her oldest sister, dead air came from the radio station she was listening to. A song didn't play. Finally, the voice of the afternoon DJ came though the radio's speaker.

"Ladies and gentlemen, I don't know how to tell you this. I don't know how to say it," he said.

The DJ's voice broke. Jennie could tell he was struggling not to cry.

"I just received this bulletin and I just don't...I just don't believe it," he said, then took a huge pause.

Jennie's heart rate climbed instantly. What had happened? Could the president have been shot? Oh no. Had someone assassinated President Carter?

Finally, the DJ broke the news.

"Ladies and gentlemen...Elvis Presley is dead."

His words hung in the silent air that followed this announcement.

"What?" Jennie said. This couldn't be true.

She clutched her stomach and the child within with one hand. With the other she covered her mouth, holding back what might be ready to come out of her.

"There's not much information here," the DJ said. "Elvis was rushed to Baptist Hospital in Memphis, where police say he died of respiratory failure."

The DJ paused again. When he spoke next, he was crying.

"Ladies and gentleman, at the age of forty-two, the King of Rock and Roll is dead."

As the DJ openly sobbed over the radio waves, Jennie did the same, slowly sinking to her knees. Elvis couldn't be dead. He couldn't be. She'd just met him. He'd shown her such kindness and generosity. Everything in the baby's room was because of the money he'd tipped her that night.

But now he was gone. Elvis was dead.

How could such a kind, sweet, and generous man die at such a young age?

Jennie put her hand in her face and wept, just as many people across America and the world were now doing as they learned of Elvis's passing on August 16, 1977.

But Jennie wouldn't remember that day solely for the grief caused by his sudden death.

In the midst of her tears, Jennie's water broke.

CHAPTER 5

March 20, 2017

THINGS HADN'T WORKED OUT AS Randall Briggs had planned.

Not in any aspect of his life.

Randall refused to believe smoking caused lung cancer. Yet here he sat with clear plastic tubes up his nose and the canister of oxygen on the floor beside his chair. Two marriages hadn't succeeded either. He had one daughter whom he'd never met. Ex-wife Number Two had split on him while still expecting, not wanting to raise a child with Randall.

On top of that, he'd never been able to unload that damned Elvis jumpsuit.

Randall had gotten away with the theft that night forty years ago, but the next day, all hell had broken loose. Elvis and his people knew the jumpsuit was missing. They suspected it had been stolen when they went to the movies.

Many of the hotel's employees could have done it, but Randall was the only person known to have gone into the suite when it was unoccupied. Although he denied it, all suspicion fell upon him. Since the jumpsuit was never recovered, the manager fired Randall, hoping to appease Elvis and his people.

Randall had always hated that stupid job. He should have been glad to be gone, but he hated it even more that no one believed he might be innocent. Yes, he'd stolen the jumpsuit, but he could not tolerate when people didn't trust him. He figured he'd lie low and sell it in a few months.

But then that damned Elvis up and died.

His death hadn't surprised Randall at all. The Elvis he'd met that summer wasn't the Elvis from the black-and-white TV shows or all those stupid movies. The Elvis he'd encountered was a fat, sweaty, disgusting mess.

And, as Randall had predicted, those drugs he'd found in the shaving kit had taken Elvis out. On the crapper too! Randall laughed at the notion that the King had died on his throne.

The hysteria over Elvis's death had been intense. Elvis records and memorabilia flooded nearly every store. People could not get enough of the now-dead singer. Randall could only imagine how much someone might now pay for the jumpsuit he'd taken as his enhanced tip.

And that was how it remained. Randall could only imagine his payday.

Before he could find a way to sell it, Randall received a visit from a private investigator working for the Presley estate.

"I'm attempting to locate a jumpsuit that belonged to Elvis. It went missing here in Springfield during the final weeks of his last tour," the PI said.

"I've been accused forever of taking that thing. Even lost my job because of it," Randall said.

"I know that. It's why I'm here," the PI said in a matter-of-fact tone.

"I wouldn't take that damn thing, nor would I want to," Randall said, one of thousands of times he'd said it since stealing the jumpsuit that June. It miffed him that one would take his word on the matter.

"I understand that, Mr. Briggs. But if you did know where it might be and helped me recover it, Elvis's estate would be very happy. And there wouldn't be any questions asked about how you helped me out."

Randall shook his head. Elvis may be dead, but his cheapness remained. If they offered him a thousand-dollar reward or something like that, he'd help the PI find it. But he didn't, so Randall wouldn't.

"Well, I can't help you out 'cause, as I already told you, I don't have a clue where that damn thing might be."

"I'm supposed to believe that, Mr. Briggs?"

"I don't give a hot damn what you believe or don't. Now get off my property."

Randall stepped back inside his mobile home and slammed the door in the PI's face.

The PI knocked on the door for about five minutes. Randall ignored him, and finally the man went away. Randall hoped that would be the last he'd hear from the estate. As usual, his hopes didn't wind up matching with reality.

Once a year or so, Randall would receive a letter from the estate's lawyers and sometimes a visit from other PIs. They remained convinced he possessed the missing jumpsuit. Randall always denied their accusations, and they could never prove he was lying.

This had the unfortunate consequence of preventing Randall from ever profiting from the late Elvis's jumpsuit. Even when the internet came alive and the online auction of eBay was only a few mouse clicks away, Randall couldn't risk trying to sell the damned thing.

Finally, however, things changed, but not exactly for the better.

Randall Briggs was dying and, as always, needed money.

But he didn't need it for any creature comforts. No, Randall needed cash for his funeral. There wouldn't be anyone to bury him. Like with everything else in his life,

Randall had to take care of himself. So now, after all these years, he was taking the chance of selling the jumpsuit to afford a burial plot in the cemetery where generations of his kin rested. And since he'd never owned anything nice in this life, Randall figured he'd buy a nice coffin for his journey to the next.

Randall heard a car pull up outside and took a long drag his cigarette. He rose from his well-worn La-Z-Boy chair. It took great strength from him to even do that. He pulled the blinds aside and saw a black Dodge Charger in the parking spot beside his mobile home.

The man from Hollywood had arrived.

CHAPTER 6

THE MAN FROM HOLLYWOOD WASN'T in the movie industry. Cameron Edmund Ogilvie's business was music. He'd made a career of finding hot, unknown new acts, making them superstars, and wringing every cent out of their recordings and performances before their fans tired of them and moved on to next hot thing.

But if things worked out for him today in this godforsaken place, he wouldn't have to worry about the expiration date of his performers and their dwindling profitability. Those days would long be over. On top of that, Cameron would make music history and be remembered forever.

Those thoughts excited Cameron. He was eager to get out of the back of the rented Dodge Charger. Fatu, his stocky Samoan bodyguard and driver, took his sweet, deliberate time, as usual, to get out and open the door.

"Dammit. Can't you move any faster, fathead?" Cameron said as Fatu opened the car's rear door.

Fatu did not respond to the insult. He never did. He seldom spoke, which was exactly the way Cameron liked it.

Cameron climbed out of the Charger into the trailer park. He surveyed his surroundings and wondered if the place had at one point been hit by a tornado and never repaired. Who knew and who cared?

As Cameron approached the steps to Randall Briggs's trailer, the door opened and Randall stepped out.

Cameron gave Randall the once-over. Randall appeared to be a living white-trash cliché, residing in a trailer park and chain-smoking despite the oxygen tubes shoved up his nostrils because he could no longer breathe. Cameron made a mental note to scrub his hands with sanitizer when he returned to the car.

"You Cameron Ogilvie?" Randall asked.

"Yes. I'm Mr. Ogilvie," Cameron said. He hated when people he wasn't friends with called him by his common name. And he wasn't friends with many people.

Randall put his cigarette in his mouth, freeing his right hand so he could shake Cameron's.

"That's probably not the best idea," Cameron said.

"No reason to quit now. Not like they can reverse what I got."

"That's not exactly what I meant," Cameron said. He pointed to the green oxygen tank and the *flammable* warning painted on its side.

Randall took a deep drag and smiled. "Don't worry. I don't plan to blow you up before you've paid me."

"Then let me see what you say you have for sale."

Randall led Cameron inside. Cameron's skin tightened being in this repulsive environment. He followed Randall through the living room of battered and worn-out furniture, where empty beer cans and discarded packages of microwave dinners abounded in the open spaces.

Randall stopped in the hallway and opened a small closet. He pulled the brass chain hanging down from the ceiling. The light came on. Randall stepped aside and Cameron stepped into the small closet. A bulging garment bag hung in the closet.

Cameron's anticipation and excitement grew. He took the bag off its rack. Slowly, he unzipped it. Inside the garment bag, he discovered a white jumpsuit adorned with numerous rhinestones. It had definitely been designed in the flamboyant and gaudy style of Elvis Presley.

This could really be it, Cameron thought. The rumored missing jumpsuit that Elvis's estate denied even existed. They'd gone so far to tell people that in the last year of his life, Elvis could only fit into one of his jumpsuits on his final tour. That one was now on display at Graceland. The other one—its twin—had allegedly gone missing after a concert here in Springfield, Missouri. Could this be it?

Cameron pulled the bag completely off the jumpsuit. He knew instantly that this was the genuine article. This had belonged to Elvis. The King of Rock and Roll had worn it. But was there any Elvis on it? That was what Cameron needed to know more than anything else.

He examined the oversize collar. That would be the best place for him to look. Yes. There it was! Resting on the inside of the collar at the back of the neckline lay a hair follicle.

"When and where did you get this?" Cameron asked.

"I already told you," Randall said.

"Tell me again."

"Springfield. June of '77. The night he played at the university."

Cameron's eyes narrowed as he stared at Randall.

"And how exactly did *you* wind up with it?"

"I didn't steal it," Randall said, sticking to his lie.

"Of course you didn't, but if you expect me to purchase it, then first I want to know how it wound up here with you."

"Let's say he should've tipped me better than a measly hundred dollars."

Cameron smiled. While many people foolishly looked down upon greed, he admired that trait in a man. It showed they had drive and wouldn't take no for an answer. Perhaps if Randall Briggs had been a little greedier, he wouldn't have ended up in this pathetic trailer park.

Cameron turned and nodded to Fatu, who stood dutifully by the front door. Fatu received the silent instruction and went outside.

Cameron smiled at Randall Briggs.

"Mr. Briggs, we definitely have ourselves a deal."

"I'm glad to hear that."

"Oh, I'm sure you are."

Fatu returned a minute later with a black leather briefcase. He brought it to Cameron and held it flat, his forearms under it providing a surface. Cameron rolled the combination locks to their numbers then unlatched the case. Inside sat numerous packets of hundred-dollar bills.

Cameron counted out then handed over ten thousand in cash to Randall, then closed the case.

Randall stood mesmerized by the enormous amount of cash in his hands. Cameron noticed a tiny bit of drool forming in the corners of the dying man's mouth.

Cameron picked up the garment bag containing his purchase and headed to the door behind Fatu.

"Don't spend it all in the same whorehouse," Cameron said as he headed out.

"Hey, I'm not the kind of man who pays for it," Randall said, lying once again to defend his reputation from this Hollywood big shot.

At the doorway, Cameron turned back to Randall.

"Of course you do. We all pay for the things we want because we also know that everyone has a price."

Cameron didn't wait for a reply. He had what he'd come here for, and Randall had gotten exactly what he wanted. There was no further business to conduct here. The sooner he was out of this pit and away from Randall Briggs, the better Cameron would feel. He stepped out of the trailer and followed Fatu to the trunk of the car.

The great prize he'd been seeking for so long—a strand

of Elvis's hair—he now had in his possession. He had Elvis Presley's DNA. Now he needed to put his plan into action, but there was only one person who had the ability to help him with that.

CHAPTER 7

"CORNELIUS, AS YOU CAN SEE, is a very well-trained chimp," Dr. Victoria Hadley said into the microphone on the table before her.

Cornelius was also a hundred times more intelligent than those she was making this presentation to, she thought, but dared not say aloud.

Victoria had presented and defended her work before the world's greatest minds, researchers making groundbreaking strides, and some of the richest people on the planet.

Today, though, she had to explain her work and grovel before intellectual lightweights whose loud opinions seldom had anything to do with solid scientific facts. But that was what scientists were required to do when their research needed funding from the United States Congress. They went to Capitol Hill.

Victoria sat at the witness table facing the twelve members of the House's Committee on Science, Space, and Technology who had bothered to attend the hearing. Only eight people sat in the seats in the gallery behind her. Twenty years ago, her presentation would have been the biggest story of the week. But with Neil Gorsuch, the new president's nominee for the Supreme Court, having his hearing before the Senate Judiciary Committee at the same time, advances in cloning didn't make the headlines they once did.

The video Victoria brought played on the committee

room's monitors. She explained what the committee members, their staff, and interested media people were seeing. On screen, a chimpanzee communicated with Victoria using sign language.

"We extracted a hair follicle from Cornelius to create a genetically identical copy of him. Using an experimental growth-enhancement procedure, Cornelius's clone was effectively born at the same age as him."

The image changed to show the committee members a microscopic needle sticking into a strand of the chimp's hair. The next image revealed the needle dropping something too small for the unaided human eye to see into a transparent sac made of some unknown tissue.

The image changed to that of a chimpanzee fetus growing inside a sac of translucent fluid. Through time-lapse video, the fetus matured into a baby chimp, then into an adolescent. Finally, it had grown to be an adult chimpanzee.

In the next set of recorded images, Victoria cleaned gelatinous goo off the new chimpanzee who had emerged from the sac. The video then cut to her conversing in sign language with the cloned chimp. He signed his responses to her as easily as Cornelius had.

Then the two chimps appeared on the screen together. They looked at each other, completely identical and each mystified by the other.

"What I believe the committee will find fascinating is that not only were we able to create a clone physically identical to the original at the time we extracted the DNA, but Galen came out of the womb knowing everything we'd already taught Cornelius—including American Sign Language."

"This is extremely fascinating, Dr. Hadley," Congressman Rasp, the Republican chairman from Texas, said into his microphone. "But I'd like you to clarify something. You said Galen came out of the womb? Does that mean he was born?"

"Allow me to clarify, Mr. Chairman," Victoria said. "I refer to the growth chamber we've constructed from organic material as such simply because it literally serves the purpose of a womb in the cloning process. All other clones that have been produced have been required to be carried in the womb of a living host."

"Thank you for that clarification," Rasp said. "Now, are there any other ways that the cloning process is different?"

"As you can see, the genetic growth enhancers allowed us to accelerate the aging process so that Galen came forth completely identical, including in biological age, as Cornelius. Also, whereas Cornelius can procreate naturally, Galen is sterile."

"And was that intentional?"

"It wasn't, and the reason for it isn't entirely clear at this point. It could have something to do with the growth enhancers. It might also be something we don't yet understand about replicating primates. This is something I intend to delve into in my next round of research."

"Thank you, Dr. Hadley," Rasp said. "I reserve the balance of my time and will turn things over to the ranking member."

Constance Cleary, the top Democrat on the committee, pulled her mic closer to her mouth.

"Thank you, Mr. Chairman," Cleary said. "Dr. Hadley, your research and results here are truly phenomenal. Now that you've been able to successfully clone a chimpanzee, how much more work do you believe needs to be done before you would be able to clone a human being?"

"Cloning Cornelius was a major undertaking that only happened after years of unsuccessful attempts," Victoria said. "And while this is a great leap forward in the field, as humans and chimpanzees share ninety-six percent of the same DNA, as I indicated, more research needs to be done before attempting to replicate a human being."

"Could you give us your best estimate as to how long before someone like yourself might be able to create a human clone?"

"With proper funding, I believe we could see a human clone by the end of the decade, if not sooner."

"And is that your goal, Dr. Hadley, to clone a human being?"

Victoria needed to be careful here, and she knew it.

"Despite the success with Cornelius and Galen, there are still many variables. I don't know if we'll ever be able to conceive a human being in a laboratory setting."

"*Conceive* a human being? Is that what you'd consider cloning, the act of conception?"

Uh-oh. Victoria knew she had stumbled with her word choice.

"Perhaps that's not the most appropriate word," Victoria said.

Congressman Rasp grabbed his microphone.

"No, let's stick with it," he said. "In your experience, when does the conception of a primate—or, hypothetically, a human being—occur in the cloning process?"

"I'm probably not the best person to answer that," Victoria said as she shifted in the wooden chair.

Rasp sat up taller. "Given the breakthroughs you just reported to our committee, I can't think of a better person to answer it. In your cloning process, have you been able to determine that life does indeed begin at the point of conception?"

Cleary jumped into the exchange.

"Mr. Chairman, it is absolutely inappropriate for you to misuse today's proceedings to grandstand in an effort to abolish a woman's constitutionally protected reproductive rights."

Rasp fired back at Cleary without hesitation. "First of all, no such right exists either in the Constitution or in nature. Life begins at conception, and the witness, definitely an expert in such matters, just testified to that."

"I don't believe she did," Cleary said, and turned her eyes to Victoria. "Or is that your testimony, Dr. Hadley?"

All attention from the committee members and from those sitting in the gallery fell squarely on Victoria.

"Actually, Ms. Cleary, I reiterated that I don't believe I'm qualified to weigh in on the issue."

Rasp said, "But, Dr. Hadley, you're creating life in your laboratory. Does that life begin the moment you conceive it in one of your artificial wombs, or is that not the case?"

Victoria took a long breath as she calculated her answer. She could see her needed funding vanishing before her eyes. If she had any chance of keeping it alive, it all depended on what she said now.

"I wouldn't use those words per se—" Victoria said.

"Then when does a clone start living?" Rasp asked.

Rasp, Cleary, and all of the other committee members stared directly at Victoria. She had no alternative but to tell them precisely what she had seen in her lab.

"By my observations, a clone's life begins when the replication process commences," she said.

"In other words, life begins at the time of conception," Rasp said. He smiled, and at Cleary beside him. "Does the ranking member have any other questions?"

Cleary thought for a moment.

"Dr. Hadley, while I am legitimately fascinated with your work," she said, "I believe you are treading on dangerous ground. Ground that could be used to undermine the advances made by women in the area of reproductive rights these last fifty years. There are simply too many unknowns surrounding your work. I don't believe I'm going to be able to support your funding request at this time."

CHAPTER 8

VICTORIA COULDN'T WAIT TO GET off Capitol Hill.

The committee hearing had blown up in her face. She never should have made the request for the twenty million dollars. Her time would have been better spent soliciting private donations. She hurried down the corridor, heading for the nearest exit, where she could get a ride that would take her straight to Dulles and on her flight back home to Los Angeles.

"For as intelligent as you are, you really blundered straight into the most contentious cultural issue of our era back there," a male said from behind.

Victoria stopped. She didn't need to look to see who had spoken. It belonged to the person she despised most on the planet, Cameron Ogilvie.

"Did you really take time out of whatever talent you're currently exploiting to come here and gloat in my rejection?" she asked.

"Victoria, I'd never gloat over your defeat," Cameron said, and walked closer to her.

"Caring and considerate. I don't remember the last time I saw that side of you."

"Hold your fire," he said, holding his hands up. "I come waving a white flag."

"If you need directions on where to stick that, I'd be happy to provide them. But I don't have time. I have a plane to catch."

"Oh, don't fly commercial. Come back to LA with me on my jet."

"I'd rather be strip-searched for ten hours by the TSA."

"Well, if that's that what gets you going these days..."

Victoria turned and headed for the exit again.

"At least hear the proposal I have for you," Cameron called after her.

"I'm not interested," she said without turning around.

"Even if I'm offering to fund the entire next phase of your research?"

She stopped, but did not turn to face him.

"That's right," Cameron said, walking up to her. "I'm willing to put up the twenty million you came her to beg these imbeciles for."

Victoria turned to face Cameron, a mixture of skepticism and anger on her face.

"And why exactly would you do that?"

"Because I want to support the groundbreaking research."

Victoria blurted out a laugh.

Cameron did not share her amusement. "Does that mean you're turning down my contribution to your work?"

She wanted to say that was exactly what she was doing. She didn't want his money. Not in a billion years. But she knew it might take her that long to raise the funds privately.

"I'm sure there are plenty of strings attached," she said.

"I wouldn't want to see my contribution squandered."

"Dammit, just tell me what you want."

"Then you do want to hear my proposal?"

"I'm still here, aren't I?"

Cameron smiled broadly. "You're going to absolutely love it."

"Then hurry up and spit it out or I'm leaving."

"Not here," Cameron said. He looked at the ceiling and the walls with suspicion. "There's probably a dozen people listening to us already."

Her patience neared its end with him. "Look—" she said, but he cut her off.

"Let's get on the plane and head west. I'll explain it all to you there. Better yet, I'll show you."

CHAPTER 9

"I DIDN'T GET ON YOUR plane to visit Vegas," Victoria told Cameron. "And I certainly didn't come to see some wannabe pretending to be Elvis."

Instead of flying to Los Angeles, Cameron had instructed his pilots take them to Las Vegas. Victoria complained, but he kept telling her, "You'll see."

He said it again as he led her into the Grand Showroom of the Oasis Hotel and Casino. Cameron showed an usher his tickets and they were led to their seats in the rear of the auditorium. On their table stood a brochure for *One Night with Elvis*.

"This is the hottest show in town right now," Cameron said as he took his seat.

Victoria didn't sit. She turned back for the doors.

"I'll find my own flight back to LA," she said.

"Stay for the show," he said before she could walk away. "Then it'll make absolute sense why we're here."

The houselights dimmed then flashed back to full brightness. Victoria looked to the main doors. A larger number of people now entered. They hurried to find their seats. She'd be a salmon swimming against the current if she tried to leave now.

Against her better judgment for the second time that day, Victoria took a seat next to Cameron. She pointed out how far they were from the stage.

"Don't have enough pull here to get you front-row seats?" she asked.

"This is a much better vantage point to watch the crowd."

"Watch the crowd? Not the show?"

"Oh, the show is fantastic. But it's the audience that has me captivated."

Before Victoria could probe his comment further, the houselights went down, sending the ballroom into complete darkness. The people seated around them went wild clapping and screaming.

The curtain parted and the spotlight fell on a lone singer with a guitar. The young man portrayed Elvis Presley in his late teens. He strummed the opening chords of "That's All Right."

He performed the song and the audience cheered its approval at the end.

The young Elvis impersonator appeared bashful, almost ashamed of their applause.

"Good evening, ladies and gentlemen…my name is Elvis Presley."

The audience went wild, reacting the way countless crowds of fans had for the real Elvis for so many years.

"That was the first song I recorded for Mr. Sam Phillips at Sun Records in Memphis, Tennessee," he said. "I don't think any of us had a clue what would happen after it was cut. Some people say it changed music. I don't know about that, but it certainly changed my life."

The young impersonator played several songs Elvis had recorded for Sun Records and then for RCA, starting with his number one hit "Heartbreak Hotel." The hits of Elvis's early career followed, but then the young man stopped performing.

"But this was 1958 and the Cold War was running pretty

hot, so naturally I was drafted to do my time in the Army for a couple years. But just like General MacArthur, I'd return."

The second act started with a new Elvis, an older impersonator marching out on stage in a green Army fatigues singing "G.I. Blues." This adult Elvis proceeded to sing several of the songs recorded during Elvis's now joked about movie career.

"The movie business ran its course and I knew there was only one thing to do, and that was to go back on TV just as I'd done all them years ago," the second impersonator told the assembled fans.

This Elvis changed into a totally black leather outfit. He sang "Guitar Man" and then switched into a white suit to sing "If I Can Dream."

"That was the beginning of the next phase of my career," Adult Elvis said. "The one that brought me to a stage just like this at another hotel not far from here."

Elvis left the stage and was replaced a moment later by a third impersonator. This one was older, fuller, and mature. He wore a rhinestoned and bellbottomed one-piece white jumpsuit as Elvis had in the 1970s. He portrayed mature Elvis, the look etched into popular culture as the last way Elvis would be remembered before his death.

Mature Elvis came to the stage signing "Burning Love," and the crowd went insane at the karate moves and wild gyrations this impersonator displayed as he sang.

Victoria looked over at Cameron. He was smiling as he watched the reaction of the crowd. He noticed her looking at him and smiled back.

"Elvis is in the building," he said.

CHAPTER 10

MICHAEL PRESCOTT WRAPPED UP "BURNING Love" and went directly into "Suspicious Minds." The fans in the darkened auditorium howled with happiness and delight. Michael ate it all up. He always did.

Michael Prescott, after all, had been born to be Elvis.

Michael had never seen Elvis perform live. He was only thirty-nine, and had not been alive when Elvis had been. Not even for a few hours. He'd been born the same day Elvis died—August 16, 1977—but at night.

That bizarre coincidence of their birth and death dates aligning had tied Michael to Elvis his entire life. When his friends were going to Pearl Jam concerts and mourning the death of Kurt Cobain, Michael was watching videos of Elvis from the 1950s and studying the life of the late King of Rock and Roll.

During his teenage years, Michael practiced sounding like Elvis in both speech and song. And he did. It was uncanny. He'd dyed his hair black and grown out his sideburns, just as Elvis had. But he didn't look enough like his idol. Michael had inherited his Roman nose from his father, and that threw the illusion off. At the age of twenty-one, though, he'd saved enough money for a nose job. He told the surgeon to give him "a nose just like Elvis's."

It worked, and Michael Prescott had made his way to Las Vegas, determined to bring Elvis Presley back to life. He instinctively knew there were multitudes of fans who still couldn't get enough of the leg-shaking, lip-curling hillbilly cat who had made rock and roll a worldwide force in music.

In his twenties, Michael had been able to bring to life the young Elvis that Sam Phillips had discovered and Tom Parker had turned into a worldwide phenomenon. As he entered his thirties, Michael transitioned into the movie years, and now, as he approached forty, he was bringing the touring Elvis of the 1970s back to life.

But unlike Elvis, Michael had obsessively taken good care of himself. He worked out every day and seldom drank. He'd avoided all drugs growing up. Bill Clinton may have lied about never inhaling a puff of marijuana, but for Michael, that was the truth. For obvious reasons, the death of Elvis had always haunted him. Michael wanted to ensure that not only would he keep the King alive, but he'd manage to stay alive longer himself.

Michael had developed the idea for *One Night with Elvis* while reflecting back on his career as a tribute artist. He'd approached two other talented tribute artists, Ty Vandekamp and Eddie Zee, with the concept. Ty channeled Elvis from the '50s, and Eddie the '60s. Together, the trio could bring the full career of Elvis to the stage. They loved the idea.

Michael then approached the Oasis Casino with his idea, and they were fully supportive. Since opening night, it had been selling out.

He knew that if he remained in shape and kept eating right, he could channel Elvis for many years to come. Now, as the highest paid tribute artist not only in Las Vegas, but the world, Michael Prescott's life could not have been better.

Little did he know that the reactions to his show and his performance as Elvis had given Cameron Ogilvie the wildest idea he'd ever thought up.

CHAPTER 11

MICHAEL CLOSED OUT THE EVENING'S show exactly as Elvis had done hundreds of times throughout the 1970s, by singing "Can't Help Falling in Love."

Even though the show ended, the audience refused to leave. They loved him and couldn't get enough. Ty Vandekamp and Eddie Zee returned to the stage and took a bow with Michael. The crowd continued to stand, clapping, screaming, and yelling.

A bra flew up and landed at the feet of the three impersonators. Michael picked it up and wiped the sweat from his brow. The audience went into a wilder frenzy.

Cameron, like the rest of those in attendance, was on his feet, clapping his hands. He turned to Victoria, who remained seated.

"Look at them!" he said. "They don't want to leave! They want more!"

Victoria stood, picking up her purse as she did. He'd pushed her patience to the edge.

"I'll admit, it's a great show, but if you don't tell me exactly what you want from me, then I'm out of here."

Cameron gestured to the screaming people surrounding them. "This is the deal. Look around you. This is my proposal."

She looked around at the members of the cheering crowd.

"Can't you see? They're all crazy about Elvis," Cameron said. "And he's been dead and rotting in his grave forty years. But they still love him. The blue-hairs who saw the real thing are here. So are their kids. Look, nearly a third of this audience is whiny millennials who never knew Elvis when he was alive."

Victoria shook her head and started for the door. "I'm done with you and your stupid games," she said.

Cameron grabbed her by the elbow. "This isn't a game," he said.

"Let go of me." She pulled away from his grip.

"Victoria, don't you understand? These are the people who are going to fund the next phase of your work. They want Elvis. And you and I going to give him back to them."

Victoria began to object, but stopped as Cameron pulled the clear plastic vial from his coat pocket. He held it up before her eyes.

The vial contained a single long strand of black hair.

"What is that?" she asked.

"Exactly what you think it is."

"It can't be."

"Oh, trust me, it is."

"How did you get it?"

"That's not important. What we're going to do with it is."

Victoria took the vial from him. She closed her right eye, held the vial up close to her left eye, and examined the hair.

"You're certain this was from Elvis?" she asked.

"Positively positive," Cameron said.

Could it be? Could this really be a hair follicle from Elvis Presley? If so, had it been preserved well enough to contain a usable piece of his DNA?

Victoria wanted to be back in her lab or, at the very least, have a powerful enough microscope to have a proper look at the strand of hair.

"This is insane," she said.

"The most revolutionary ideas always are."

"There's no way the FDA will approve the cloning of a human being, especially in this political environment."

"Screw the FDA," Cameron said as he took the vial from her hand.

"As a scientist, there are rules I must follow."

Cameron pushed air threw his lips, making a *pfft* sound. "Rules are made to be broken."

"No. This could get me into a lot of trouble. You too."

"Forgiveness is always easier to ask for than permission."

"Stop with the clichés," she said. "I'm serious."

Cameron stepped closer and looked Victoria directly in her eyes.

"Do you think I would've spent the last three years trying to track down a sample of his DNA if I wasn't serious?"

"I'm certain you're quite serious about the money you think you'll be able to make off something like this."

"Oh yes, the root of all evil. Who's using clichés now? Besides, if it wasn't for the money, we both know you wouldn't be here right now."

"I'm interested in the benefits that cloning could have for humanity," she said.

"And I thought you'd done all this for personal reasons."

Victoria looked down at the carpet. She didn't want to go there. Not with him.

"Sometimes they overlap," she said.

"As they do in this instance."

Victoria turned her attention back to the hair in the vial. He plucked it out of her hand.

"I know you," Cameron said, returning the vial to his inside coat pocket. "I know you want to do this. I know you have to do this."

"I testified under oath to Congress today that I wasn't

working on any human cloning."

"At the time you testified, you weren't."

"A technicality."

"Yet still the truth. Victoria, you are on the cusp of revolutionizing genetic science. You're closer than anyone to cloning a human being. Don't stop now. Finish this journey you're on. Let's put the past behind us and change the future together."

As self-serving as he was, he was also right. She couldn't turn back now. She'd come too far. Still, she wasn't sure it would work. As she'd testified at Capitol Hill, there were still many unknown variables to be overcome.

Yet attempting this, even if unsuccessful, would be another giant step forward in her research. It would move the possibility of human cloning, the possibility of bringing him back, closer to reality than ever before.

"I need you to take me back to LA," she said.

"I knew you'd do it."

"I didn't say that. I don't know if we can. The genetic structure of the hair may be too damaged to extract usable DNA from it."

For the first time today, she noticed a small crack in Cameron's confidence.

"And that means exactly what in English?"

"It means I'm not sure I can clone you a copy of Elvis from this hair."

CHAPTER 12

"DAMMIT, CAMERON, YOU NEED TO back off," Victoria said as she attempted to examine the alleged strand of hair under the lens of her powerful transmission electron microscope in her lab. Cameron leaned into her as he tried to get a look himself.

That morning, she'd flown back to Los Angeles with Cameron and Fatu. His plane had landed at Van Nuys Airport, where one of his cars was waiting for them. Cameron instructed Fatu to drive them directly to the Bio-Design offices in Westwood, where Victoria could properly inspect the hair follicle.

Cameron had insisted that everything they were doing be kept absolutely secret. Victoria assured him that wouldn't be a problem. She'd laid off the remaining members of her staff three months ago when her funding dried up. She was the only employee of Bio-Design today, and not even taking a paycheck for her work.

The need for funding was why she'd gone back to Washington. It was why she'd agreed to get on the plane with Cameron the day before. It was also why she was here in her lab with Cameron and Fatu.

"Is it going to work or not?" Cameron asked.

"There's been serious degradation of the cell structure," Victoria said as she did her best to keep her attention focused on the hair.

"What does that mean? Can it be done or not?" he asked.

"There really isn't much for us to work with here," Victoria said.

"Then this has all been just a waste," Cameron said in disgust. He finally stepped back from her. He kicked a chair and sent it tumbling across the room.

Victoria ignored him and continued to stare into the microscope.

"Wait," she finally said. "There might be something at the top of the follicle."

Cameron rushed up behind her again.

"What? What's at the top of it?" Cameron said.

Victoria moved aside. Cameron put his eyes to the lenses of the microscope.

"What am I looking at?" he asked.

"The narrow top of the hair. The structure of the genome there appears to be mostly intact."

"Then we can clone him," Cameron said, more as a declaration then as a question.

"The material could be sufficient enough to extract suitable DNA and attempt to replicate him, but…"

Cameron pulled up from the microscope.

"But?" he said, staring at Victoria. "I don't like that word."

"We're only going to get one shot at this," she said. "There's not enough genetic material here to successfully attempt more than one replication."

"Then I expect you to get it right," Cameron said.

"I understand that, but—"

"There's that damned word again," he said.

"—your expectations need to have a conversation with reality. Human cloning, even in the most ideal circumstances, is only a theory. And the material you've provided is far from ideal."

"Then perhaps I should take this hair and my money and find a better scientist."

"If there was one, you wouldn't have tracked me down in Washington and you wouldn't be here now."

Cameron smiled. "I certainly wouldn't be. How long will it take you to get started?

"Before I can do anything, you need to provide the funds I'm going to need."

"I'll have them wired today."

"I'm not starting until the transfer is completed."

"You really don't trust me."

"I learned my lesson."

Cameron turned away from her and pulled out his cell phone. "I'll make the call right now."

"And I'm going to need one more thing," Victoria said.

"I think twenty million is more than enough."

"It's not about the money. I need you to stay out of here while I'm working."

"I think my investment should allow me whatever access I desire," Cameron said.

"It'll be impossible for me to get any work done with you hovering around and interrupting me every five seconds," Victoria said. "If you want me to create a clone of Elvis, then transfer the money and stay out of my lab."

PART II

ALL SHOOK UP

CHAPTER 13

CAMERON HAD RELUCTANTLY AGREED TO Victoria's demand that she be left alone to do her work. However, he insisted on being nearby. He commandeered one of the vacant offices at Bio-Design, where he could attend to his other business matters.

Fatu positioned himself in the lobby, standing in the corner rather than sitting on the leather couch. He stood there silently whenever Cameron didn't need him, reading a book on a Kindle. Victoria was curious what he might be reading, but decided against asking him. Everything she'd seen about Fatu told her he wasn't the talkative type.

With both of them out of the way, Victoria sequestered herself in her lab, only to emerge to use the restroom, grab something to eat, or catch a few hours of sleep. Her first and only priority was to create a human clone, a clone of Elvis Presley.

First, Victoria extracted the genome from the strand of hair. She put the DNA into an incubation tube she'd prepared. She then inserted the genome into an egg cell and began the replication process. Within a day, an embryo had formed. After verifying the stability of the embryo, she transferred it into an awaiting organic chamber that she'd perhaps unwisely dubbed "the womb." Next, she injected the growth enhancers into the womb. In less than an hour, the monitors detected a heartbeat.

The clone had come to life at its earliest stages.

Victoria knew from her previous work on canines and primates that this accomplishment did not mean there was a perfect replica of the host subject. DNA was tricky, and there were problematic genetic codes, some incomplete and others out of sequence, that could interfere in the cloning process. Such random and unpredictable variations created mutations and defects that in the best-case scenarios would create an imperfect copy, or in the worst lead to the death of the cloned subject.

With this being her first attempt to duplicate a human, Victoria feared there might be many more unknown genetic variables than she had encountered before. After running a series of tests, she was relieved there were not any noticeable alterations in the genetic structure.

The clone of Elvis grew rapidly and without complications.

By day two, the embryo had grown into a baby boy.

On day three, he reached the size of a five-year-old child.

Victoria found a picture online of a young Elvis with his parents in Tupelo, Mississippi dating back to the 1940s. She felt encouraged. The child growing in the womb looked exactly as Elvis had appeared at the same relative age.

By the morning of day four, the clone had grown into a teenager.

That afternoon, Victoria invited Cameron to join her in the lab. It didn't surprise her at all when the silent Fatu followed his employer in too.

Fatu found a spot in the back of the room near the door to stand as Cameron hurried past Victoria toward the womb. He looked at it in awe. Inside floated a perfect clone of Elvis Aaron Presley.

The clone before him was handsome and lean as Elvis had been when entering the national consciousness in the mid-1950s.

"It's him! It's really him!" Cameron said, his excitement bursting through his typically hard and serious exterior.

He grabbed Victoria by the shoulders and kissed her on the forehead.

"You did it," he said. "I knew that you could."

"That's not quite what I remember you saying a few weeks ago," Victoria said.

"That was just the motivation. I knew you would rise to the challenge."

"You're a real Tony Robbins," she said.

"Let's pop him out of that Jell-O and welcome back the King of Rock and Roll."

"We can't," Victoria said.

Cameron spun around to her. Before he could speak, she did.

"I know you don't like the word 'can't' any more than you do the word 'but.'"

"You've got that right."

"Well, you still can't. The growth process isn't complete."

"What the hell you talking about?" Cameron said. "Look at him. It's Elvis Presley. Now get him out here and let's get him singing."

"It's not that simple," Victoria said. "The growth enhancers I've developed to accelerate the aging process must cycle through to the completion of their sequencing."

"Speak English, would you, please?"

"I can't remove him from the womb until he reaches the full maturity of the cell from which he's cloned."

Cameron rapidly processed this in his mind.

"Wait a damn minute," he said. "That hair I provided you came from Elvis in the summer of 1977, not more than a few weeks before he died."

"I know."

Victoria could see the panic on Cameron's face.

"Get him out of there," he said. "Now."

"I can't do that."

"Then I will."

Cameron moved toward the womb. He reached out to rip it open with his fingers. Victoria stepped in front of him and grabbed him by the wrists.

"Let go of me!" he said.

"Cameron, you can't just pull him out of there."

"Just watch me. Fatu!"

Fatu came forward and grabbed Victoria by the shoulders, moving her out of Cameron's way.

"Let me go!" she yelled at Fatu. Fatu kept his grip on her and said nothing.

Cameron stepped up to the womb and put his fingers into it.

"You're going to kill him!" Victoria shouted.

Cameron froze and turned his head back to Victoria for more information.

"The consequence of attempting to shortcut the enhancement sequence is fatal," she said.

Cameron weighed her statement then turned back to study the clone.

Inside the womb, fat deposits now formed on the clone's chest and stomach. The clone's face grew more rounded and a double chin started to develop.

"You don't know that," Cameron said. "You've never cloned a human before or attempted to enhance their growth. You said so yourself."

Cameron grabbed the womb again, sinking his fingers into it as he prepared to rip it open.

"Galen wasn't the first clone of Cornelius," Victoria said. "First there was Caesar, and then Milo. Caesar I removed from the womb when he reached adulthood. Unfortunately, he was a few biological years younger than Cornelius at the time. He only lived a few hours."

Cameron stopped but didn't take his fingers off the womb.

Victoria continued, "I attempted to solve the problem by removing the next clone, Milo, when he reached the biological age when a chimpanzee is born. It ended in the same result. I finally got it right with Galen."

Without looking back at her, Cameron asked, "And that means?"

"We can't remove a clone that's received growth enhancers from the womb until the sequence is complete and the clone has reached the biological age of the original's DNA from which it was replicated."

Cameron took a deep breath, closed his eyes, and shook his head over and over again.

"No," he said. "I didn't spend all this money for fat, drugged-out Elvis." He looked at the clone in the womb. "I want that Elvis. I want young, sexy, pelvis-shaking, lip-curling Elvis."

"Then you should've brought me hair from 1957 instead of 1977," Victoria said.

Cameron finally pulled his fingers away from the womb. He spun to face Victoria. His fears and anger were evident in his eyes.

"Don't try to blame me," he said as he pointed an accusing finger at her face. "This is your fault. You should have told me this before we ever started."

"We really don't have time to play the blame game," she said, looking at the digital clock on the lab's wall. "In about an hour, we're going to have a clone of Elvis Presley with us, and he's probably going to want to know what he's doing here."

CHAPTER 14

ELVIS WASN'T DEAD.

At least, he didn't think he was.

He opened his eyes with great effort. He always had a rough time waking up. There wasn't anything unusual about that. But the bright white light hanging over his face forcing him to squint was out of place.

Elvis sat up in the narrow bed his overweight body occupied and looked around. He was in a white room with only two straight-backed chairs and a table as furniture. He glanced down to find his body covered only by a sheet.

Where the heck was he? Was this a hospital? Had he gotten sick on tour?

"Good morning, Mr. Presley," a woman said. He hadn't noticed anyone else in the room.

Elvis turned his head to the left. A pretty woman wearing a white lab coat came toward him. She looked a lot like Priscilla, but it wasn't her. Behind her stood a smiling man with a hairline that had long ago retreated to the top of his head.

"How are you feeling?" she asked.

"Like I got hit head-on by a Mack truck," Elvis said. His head hurt, and he laid it back down on the pillow. "What happened to me? Where the heck am I?"

"That's a bit of the story," she said. "Perhaps the best place for us to start is if you'll tell me what the last thing you remember was."

"Uh, yeah," Elvis said. He took a few seconds to run through his memories. "I'd just finished my show in Springfield."

Elvis sat up again. He noticed a mirror on the sidewall. As was his lifelong habit, he checked himself in it. The image looking back shocked him.

His hair was a salt-and-peppered brown instead of the black he'd perpetually dyed it for the last twenty years.

Where was he? Who were these people? What had they done to him?

He looked around for his clothes. He didn't see them. His boots weren't anywhere to be seen either. If they had his clothes, then they had his guns. He was unarmed, except for his self-defense skills.

Elvis pushed himself out the bed and broke into a fighting stance. He quickly noticed he was naked, and pulled the sheet from the small bed to cover his private parts.

Elvis sized up the people in the room. The bald man closest to him probably wasn't the biggest threat. It was the stocky Islander standing behind him that would be the problem. He was the muscle. The pretty woman wouldn't make him any trouble. Besides, he'd never strike a woman.

"All right, I wanna know who the heck you people are and what I'm doing here," Elvis said.

"First of all," the woman said, "we all know who you are, but you don't know any of us. I'm Dr. Victoria Hadley, and this is Cameron Ogilvie." She pointed to the bald man, but didn't introduce the Islander fella.

Elvis asked, "If you're a doctor, that mean I get sick?"

"Not exactly," she said. "But I'm really not sure where we should start."

"Why don't you start with getting me my clothes and showing me to the front door?"

"This may be a bit difficult for you to properly comprehend," Victoria said.

Elvis didn't need them to explain. He already knew what had happened. How it happened was a bigger question, but that wasn't important now. They'd somehow managed to kidnap him, and he needed to get away.

"Elvis," the man named Cameron said, and stepped toward him.

Elvis cocked his free hand into fist. "I'm gonna warn you, pal. I'm an eighth-degree san black belt, trained by the great Master Kang Rhee himself. I don't want to hurt you, but I'll break your neck if I have to."

Cameron put his hands up. "None of us are going to hurt you," he said.

"You got that darn right. And I ain't giving you any money."

Cameron smiled. "I'm not interested in your money. I'm interested in making money with you."

"Colonel Parker handles all my business. But I doubt he'll want to be in cahoots with people like you. Now it ain't public knowledge, but I'm an undercover federal agent at large, which makes kidnapping me a federal crime."

"Yes, I'm well aware that President Nixon deputized you," Cameron said.

How the heck did this fella know about that? That was supposed to be top-top secret. Before Elvis could ask him about that, Victoria the doctor spoke again.

"We didn't kidnap you," she said.

Elvis let out a laugh. "Sure you didn't. That's why none of my fellas are here. Now you get me Charlie Hodge or Joe Esposito on the double."

"I'm afraid that's not going to be possible," Cameron said.

"Which proves you kidnapped me."

Victoria said, "You said the last thing you remember was coming back to your hotel after your show. Do you know what the date of that show was?"

"You being serious, lady?"

"Yes. I'm trying to explain what's happened here."

Elvis tried to recall the date. His memory was fuzzy. He'd done so many shows that many of the days blended into one another.

"Uh, the seventeenth," Elvis said, half guessing.

"Of what month?" she asked.

"June, of course."

"And of what year?"

"I'm done playing around like this," Elvis said.

"Please," she said. "Just tell me what year you think it is."

"Think it is? Lady, it's the year of our Lord nineteen hundred and seventy-seven. You need me to make it clearer than that?"

Victoria took a couple of tentative steps toward him.

"I know you're going to find this rather difficult to believe," she said. "But it's not."

She pointed to the calendar hanging on the wall. Elvis gave a sideways glance at it without letting the sheet or his guard down. He zeroed in on the date. For a second, it shocked him, but he recovered and smiled.

"Well, I guess this all makes sense, then," he told his captors.

"Then you do understand?" Cameron said, putting his hands down and smiling widely.

"I was wondering why there ain't no windows," Elvis said. "This has gotta be a colony on the moon."

"Oh my God," Cameron said. "He's an absolute moron."

Elvis glared at him. "What did you say?" Elvis asked, ready to pounce.

"This is not a moon colony," Cameron said.

"You sure about that?"

"Yes, because there aren't any colonies on the moon."

"I gotcha," Elvis said. "'Cause that means this ain't 2017."

"And you think that by 2017 there'll be colonies on the moon?" Cameron asked.

"They'll be there by 2001. Ain't you seen the movie?"

Victoria inched closer to him. "Okay," she said. "For the sake of argument, let's say there are settlements on the moon. If society's scientifically advanced enough to have people living on the moon, then wouldn't it also be feasible that we'd also be able to make clones of people?"

Elvis thought about this for a few seconds before answering. "You mean like making dittos of 'em?"

"Yes, exact genetic replicas of a person," Victoria said.

"I reckon so. But if you think you're gonna make a damn clone out of me, you've got another thing coming."

"No, idiot," Cameron said. "*You're* the clone."

"No, man. I'm Elvis Presley, and your face is about to be a punching bag."

Elvis started for Cameron, but Victoria stepped in his way.

"You're right," she said. "You are Elvis Presley."

"I ain't ever had a question about that," Elvis said.

"You're also an exact copy of him," she said.

Her statement confused Elvis. "So you're trying to say that I'm me but I ain't me?"

"I know it's confusing," she said. "You are Elvis, but you're also a copy of Elvis."

Elvis shook his head. These people were trying to confuse him.

"All right, I've had enough of this baloney," Elvis said.

"It's not baloney," Cameron said. "It's the truth."

"Right. I'm a ditto of Elvis. Tell you what, you go get me my clothes and let me out of here or you're going to be picking your teeth up off the floor."

"Hold on. I have an idea," Victoria said. She turned to the Islander still holding his position behind Cameron. "Fatu, can you go get the jumpsuit?"

Fatu kept his eyes on Elvis. He didn't respond to Victoria.

"Cameron," she said. "Tell him to go get it."

"We have more important issues at hand," Cameron said.

"I think this might help resolve them," she said.

Cameron took a second then nodded over his shoulder to the Islander. "Go get it," he said.

The big man named Fatu did an about face and left the room. Elvis was alone with Cameron and Victoria now.

This might be the break he needed. Elvis knew he could take down the smart-mouthed Cameron and get out before his muscle was back.

But before Elvis could take action, Fatu returned carrying a concert jumpsuit Elvis remembered wearing earlier that night.

"I guess you're not just kidnappers—you're thieves, too," Elvis said.

"It was stolen, all right," Cameron said. "But not by me. By a bellman at your hotel in Springfield who thought you didn't tip him enough."

"Now I know you're lying, 'cause I ain't ever been no cheapskate."

Victoria said, "Never mind how he obtained your jumpsuit. There was a hair follicle on the collar. I was able to take your DNA from it and make a clone. I was able to make you. And I know it's hard to believe, but you're an exact copy of him in every way up until that hair fell off on June of 1977."

Elvis nodded and smiled.

"All right, lady, if that's the story you're sticking to," Elvis said, "then where's the original me at that you say you copied me from?"

CHAPTER 15

VICTORIA PULLED HER IPHONE OUT of the side pocket of her lab coat. She went to Google and searched for the best website that would answer the clone's question.

"What are you doing?" Cameron asked.

"Answering his question," she said.

"Is that really such a good idea?" Cameron asked.

"Do you have a better one?" Victoria said.

After finding the webpage she wanted, Victoria offered the iPhone to the clone. He looked at it but did not take it from her.

"What the heck kind of TV is that?" Elvis asked.

"It's not a television. It's a phone," Victoria said.

"Oh, come on now. That little thing can't be a phone."

"It's actually a lot more than a phone," she said. "It's probably closer to a computer."

Elvis shook his head. "You know, if you wanna fool someone into believing he's in the future, you should make it more believable. A computer would be taking up the whole room we're in now, and then some."

"Just take a look at this," Victoria said as she continued to offer Elvis the phone.

"At what?" Elvis asked.

"You wanted to see where the original you is, didn't you?"

Elvis took the phone from her. She had opened the *New York Times* archive from Wednesday, August 17, 1977.

A picture of Elvis from a few years earlier and in somewhat better shape was on the left-hand side. Below it the headline read, *Elvis Presley Dies; Rock Singer Was 42.*

"Oh, so now you want me to believe I'm dead," the clone said.

"Not you, you're absolutely alive," Victoria said. "But the real you, who you remember being, he died forty years ago."

"The real me?"

Cameron spoke before Victoria could. "She means the original you, not the real you."

"Well, let me tell you something. The original me and the real me ain't dead. I'm standing right here getting fed up listening to you and your crap."

Victoria came closer, taking her iPhone back from Elvis. "I know this has to be extremely confusing. The original Elvis did die, but we were able to clone him, which is you."

His face showed the obvious confusion he was struggling with. Elvis sat down on the bed. He seemed physically pained. He closed his eyes and rubbed his forehead.

"Are you all right?" Victoria asked.

"Heck no, I ain't feeling all right." He raised a hand to hold her off, then said to himself, "Man, I gotta talk to Dr. Nick about whatever he put in my packets for this tour."

"What?" Victoria asked.

Elvis snapped, "Don't you worry about it. I just need to center my mind and get out of this hallucination."

Elvis closed his eyes again and took a deep breath.

Cameron said, "This is not a hallucination."

"Yes, it is. 'Cause I know this ain't the future and I know I sure as heck ain't dead. Just tell me what the heck you want and let me go home."

Victoria looked at Cameron. He could see she had something on her mind, but wasn't voicing it.

"What?" he asked her.

"That might not be a bad idea," Victoria said.

CHAPTER 16

CAMERON'S PLANE TOUCHED DOWN AT the Memphis airport the next morning. A car was waiting for them. Cameron, Victoria, and Elvis climbed into the back. Fatu, of course, got behind the wheel and drove.

Cameron had opposed the idea of taking Elvis to Memphis, but Victoria prevailed. She believed this would be the best way for Elvis to accept what had they had told him had happened, that he was a clone. Elvis didn't care. He had convinced them to fly him home. He'd play along with them, then, when the right time came, he planned on making a break from his three kidnappers.

But it troubled them that they had agreed to bring him to Memphis. They had to know this would be where their scheme would be foiled. Yet here they were, driving out to Graceland. Did they believe their own crazy story? If they did, then they were all definitely candidates for the loony bin. Still, something troubled him about their willingness to come here.

Elvis didn't say a word as they drove out to Graceland. The last time he'd spoken to them was during their drive to Van Nuys Airport. He complained of hunger. He hadn't eaten since hours before his show, and insisted they stop at Burger King.

Cameron protested, saying he thought Elvis needed to be careful with what he ate. Elvis hated when people talked about his weight, and continued to complain about his hunger. He told Cameron to mind his own damn business.

Victoria intervened and agreed that they should all grab something to eat. Fatu pulled into a Burger King along the way and took the car into the drive-thru window. Famished, Elvis ordered five Whoppers with bacon and extra mayo with a large Tab. The young girl working there didn't know what a Tab was. Victoria ordered him a Diet Coke.

As he'd scarfed down his food as the car drove along, Elvis noticed that nothing looked right outside. He'd spent plenty of time in Los Angeles during his career, and even had a home in Bel Air, but something was wrong. Everything seemed more crowded and brighter. The cars on the road were different. They were sleeker, smaller, and the windows even darker. Many of them, sadly, weren't even made by American companies.

He found the same to be true when he got to Memphis. Nothing seemed right there either. While it was all familiar, it didn't look quite the way he remembered it a few weeks ago when he'd been home from the road. It increased his anxiety. Elvis did his best to keep his composure and hide his rising blood pressure from the kidnappers.

When Fatu pulled the car off the freeway onto Route 51, how Elvis still thought of it even though it had been renamed Elvis Presley Boulevard years ago, his heart raced faster. He was close to home. He was anxious to walk through the doors of Graceland and get this trio in handcuffs like they belonged.

The troubling sense of uneasiness continued to grow within Elvis. He'd been up and down this road countless times since he purchased Graceland for himself and his parents back in '57. The street today was wider than he remembered, and the buildings were different. Ones that had been there forever were gone, and new ones now stood on once-vacant land.

And all up and down the road were signs and images of him.

What the heck was going on?

Off to the left, he saw the gates of Graceland and the stone fence he'd had installed after moving in.

But Fatu turned the car right instead of making a left toward the gates.

"Wait. Where are you going?" Elvis asked.

"He's parking," Cameron said.

Elvis pointed across the boulevard. "My home's right over there."

"But parking's on this side of the highway," Cameron said.

Fatu made the left into the area across the street advertising Graceland. None of this looked familiar. None of this was familiar. This wasn't real. This was all in his mind. Yeah, it was a hallucination. That was it. They must have drugged him. He had to get away from them. He had to get out. He had to do it now.

And he did.

When the car stopped, Elvis opened the door and ran for it.

"Wait," Victoria called after him. He heard her, but he wasn't listening.

There was a break in traffic on the boulevard. Elvis ran across the multi-lane road as fast as he could, which was more of a jog through quicksand than a run.

He reached the gatehouse, winded, and leaned against a stone column to catch his breath. A guard stepped out. Elvis didn't recognize the man at all.

"Can I help you, sir?" the guard asked.

"Yeah," Elvis said, taking a deep gulp of air. "I think I've been kidnapped."

"You think you've been what?"

"Kidnapped. I just got away."

"Are you all right?"

"I think so. I don't know. I think they drugged me."

"Okay. I'll give the police a call," the guard said, and headed back into his booth.

"That can wait. They're right over there."

Elvis pointed across the street at Cameron, Victoria, and Fatu crossing the boulevard.

"That's them?" the guard asked.

"Yeah. I gotta get up to the house."

"Sir, you can stay here with me, but I can't let you on the premises."

Elvis was outraged. "You telling me I can't go into my own house?"

"Your house?"

"I know they took the dye out of my hair, but can't you see it's me?"

The guard studied Elvis. "Sir, I like a good joke as much as the next guy, but if you want to visit Graceland, you need to go across the street and buy a ticket and take the tour like everyone else."

"A ticket? Man, this is my house here."

"I understand Elvis belongs to his fans," the guard explained calmly. "But Graceland is still private property. You need to go across the street and buy a ticket if you want to go inside."

Elvis couldn't believe this guy's attitude. And why didn't he even recognize him?

"Who are you?" Elvis asked. "Where's Uncle Travis? Did my daddy hire you?"

"Sir, if you're not going to buy a ticket, then you're going to need to leave."

Cameron approached Elvis. He, Victoria, and Fatu formed a semicircle around him. Victoria put a gentle hand on Elvis's bicep.

"I apologize for my friend," Cameron said to the guard. "He's just really excited to be here."

"We see plenty of fans like this every day," the guard said.

Elvis pulled away from Victoria. "I ain't a fan, dammit. I am Elvis."

He pushed the guard aside and ran through the open gates of Graceland.

"Get back here!" the guard yelled.

Elvis booked it up the driveway to the front doors of his home. He breathed heavily when he reached the other side. He definitely needed to lose some weight. But the important thing was that he'd gotten away from his kidnappers and tricked them into bringing him home. Everything would be fine now.

Elvis grabbed the handle of the front door and opened it. He stepped through and froze.

Things were wrong in his house too.

A velvet rope blocked his path to the stairs leading up to his bedroom.

"Daddy!" Elvis yelled.

No answer. He must be out.

"Dodger!" he said, knowing his grandmother would be home.

No answer again.

He called out for his cousin next. "Billy!"

Nothing. Where could everyone be?

Two security guards emerged from the kitchen.

"Just calm down, buddy," the taller guard said.

"Don't you tell me to calm down," Elvis said. "Get out of my house. You're trespassing."

"Nobody's trespassing here but you, sir," the shorter guard said as they both approached.

"How can I be trespassing at my own home?"

The taller guard moved closer to Elvis. "Sir, if you won't leave peacefully, we're going to have to detain you and call for the police."

"I'd like to see you try," Elvis said, and went into a fighting stance.

The two guards halted as Elvis threw a flurry of punches and a couple roundhouse kicks in the air. Elvis then took advantage of their hesitation and rushed out the front door.

As he came on to the front porch, he saw the guard from the gatehouse coming toward him. The three kidnappers followed behind the guard.

Elvis cut left. He'd go around by the pool and to the back of the house. There had to be someone here. Maybe Daddy was back working in the office.

Elvis made it to the side of Graceland. He was prepared to turn at the pool when two more guards came at him from the rear of the mansion. He decided to continue straight on for the Meditation Garden.

When Elvis entered the garden, he stopped cold in his tracks.

On the ground, he saw what appeared to be a grave with the name Gladys Presley engraved on it.

What was this? This wasn't where they'd buried his dear mother in 1958.

Next to that lay another grave marker.

The name on it was his father's—Vernon Presley. The date of his death was June 26, 1979.

1979? How could that be possible? That was still two years from now.

Wasn't it?

Then Elvis saw something that sent a wave of chills throughout his entire body.

Between his parents' graves was another. The tombstone

there read *Elvis Aaron Presley, January 8, 1935 – August 16, 1977.*

Elvis's mind raced as he attempted to comprehend what lay in front of his eyes. Either his kidnappers had gone to elaborate lengths with their hoax or he was having a nightmare more realistic and frightening than any he'd ever dreamed before.

But could it all be possible? Could it all be real? Was he actually dead?

His heart beat harder and faster. His lungs could barely move air in and out fast enough. He felt dizzy.

Elvis spun around, ready to run. Five guards surrounded him.

Elvis knew he could take them all, but he didn't have the strength to clench his fists, let alone raise his arms. His vision blurred. Everything around him spun in wild circles. Then blackness descended upon him.

CHAPTER 17

ELVIS OPENED HIS EYES THEN sat up in the large hotel bed with some difficulty.

Victoria offered him a glass of water. Elvis took it, gulped it down, and handed the empty glass back to her.

"Where am I?" he asked.

"The Peabody Hotel," she said.

"The Peabody? The place with the baby ducks in the fountain?"

"That's the one."

Elvis smiled. "I always liked them ducks."

"How are you feeling?" Victoria asked.

"Like I got thrown out of a speeding Cadillac." He shook his head. "Those fellows must have cold-cocked me pretty good"

"They never touched you," Elvis heard Cameron say.

Elvis looked up and found the bald, mouthy man standing at the foot of the bed. Fatu was in the room too. The big Islander stood in the corner as before, watching everything in silence.

"Then who knocked me out?" Elvis asked.

"You fainted," Victoria said.

"No. I ain't never fainted before."

"Fortunately, this time you did," Cameron said. "Otherwise, the guards might have called the police, and then we'd really have a situation to deal with."

Elvis shook his head. "No. Maybe I might've passed out, but I didn't faint. Fainting ain't real manly."

He could see Cameron was about to make a remark, but Victoria spoke first. "What's the last thing you remember before waking up right now?"

Elvis closed his eyes for a moment, then said in barely a whisper, "My grave."

Quiet filled the hotel room. Elvis didn't like that silence and decided to break it.

"So how'd it happen?" he asked.

"Well," Cameron said, "it took a while to locate an adequate sample of your DNA, but once that happened, Victoria here was able to get you back into the world pretty quick."

"No. I mean...how'd I...die?"

Cameron looked Elvis in the eye. "The official story is that you had a heart attack."

"Official story?" Elvis asked. "You mean something else happened to me?"

"Well, you did have a heart attack, but it wasn't brought on by natural causes."

"Like foul play? You saying someone poisoned me?"

"In a manner of speaking," Cameron said. "They found a lot of drugs in your system."

"That can't be," Elvis said. "I don't do drugs."

"Are you saying you weren't taking drugs?" Victoria asked him.

"No way. Now, I did take some pills, but they were all prescribed to me by Dr. Nick, and he'd never give me anything to take that was dangerous."

"That grave you saw at Graceland tells a different story," Cameron said.

Elvis sat up in the bed and pointed a finger at Cameron. "You listen here. Dr. Nick's a good man and a friend of mine. Don't you go and try to sully his name with me."

"Elvis," Cameron said, "I know you consider Dr. Nick a friend, but the pills he was giving you definitely contributed to your death."

Elvis pushed himself up and climbed out of the bed.

"The pills aren't the problem. It's everybody trying to meddle in my life and trying to tell me what to do that is."

"Keep believing that and in two months you'll be dead again," Cameron said.

Elvis took a step toward Cameron. "Listen here, man. I don't know who you are, but nobody talks to me that way."

Cameron held his hands out. "I can see how difficult it is for this to all make sense," he said. "So let's not dwell on your death. Let's look at the positive here. You've got a second chance to do things right."

A vicious verbal assault shot out of Elvis at Cameron.

"Ain't no one ever sold as many records as me! I was the highest-paid movie star in Hollywood after I got out of the Army. And I'm the only person to ever sell out the Houston Astrodome. I did things right, and if you think just 'cause you done copied me that I have to stick around and listen to this, well, y'all got another thing coming."

Elvis moved for the door. Fatu stepped in front of it.

"Oh, you want to find out how good I am?" Elvis asked, raising his fists to fight. Fatu remained silent and unmoving.

"Let him go," Victoria said.

Elvis remained staring at Fatu. Behind him, he heard Cameron say to Victoria, "If you think I'm allowing a twenty-million-dollar investment walk out the door because he's in full denial of his drug problem, then you've got another thing coming."

Hearing this, Elvis spun to face Cameron.

"I ain't your investment. And don't think I can't take both him and you. I'm an eighth-degree san black belt, trained by the great Master Kang Rhee himself."

"He just needs to blow off some steam," Victoria said to Cameron. "Besides, where does he have to go?"

Cameron was about to mouth off again. This time, Elvis was going to let him have it. He must have sensed it, as Cameron closed his mouth and nodded to Fatu. In his peripheral vision, Elvis saw Fatu step away from the door. But the Islander didn't take his eyes off Elvis.

Elvis glared at Fatu and said, "Wise decision." He kept his eyes on Fatu as he brushed past him to the door. Elvis turned the doorknob and, seconds later, was in the hallway. He slammed the door behind him.

He hurried down the hallway and found the elevator. He pressed the down button, and in about five seconds the doors opened. Elvis stepped into the elevator car and took it down to the lobby.

Stepping out, Elvis immediately recognized the lobby of the Peabody. He'd signed his contract with RCA here back in 1955 when Colonel Parker had bought out Mr. Phillips.

He saw the fountain in the center of the lobby. He smiled at memories from his younger days of the ducklings swimming in the fountain. He wondered if they still had them ducks.

"Are you okay?" a woman asked from behind him.

Elvis turned to see Victoria coming off the adjacent elevator.

"I figured he'd send Oddjob after me, not you."

"He wanted to, but I don't see how that would help."

"You're saying you came down to help me, huh?"

"Yes."

She seemed sincere. He didn't know if she was. Of the three, she'd been the kindest and most understanding to him. Still, she was mixed up with the Cameron fellow. That didn't bode well for her in Elvis's thoughts. Yet, in his life, he'd always tried not to prejudge anyone. The best way to determine her character was by giving her a chance to demonstrate it.

"All right," Elvis said. "If you want to help me, then help me get out of here."

Without hesitation, she asked, "Where do you want to go?"

Elvis thought for a moment. "Graceland," he said. "I want to go back to Graceland."

"I don't know if that's such a good idea," she said. "Besides, I'm pretty sure it's closed at this hour."

Elvis looked her in the eye. "I get it. It ain't my home no more. I just need to see it again."

Finally, Victoria nodded and pulled her portable phone out of her pocket.

"All right," she said. "I'll get us an Uber."

"A what-er?"

"It's like a taxi."

Five minutes later, Elvis climbed into the backseat of a Ford Explorer with Victoria. The driver didn't question their destination even at this late hour. And like everyone else he'd encountered, the driver didn't recognize Elvis. That, like everything else he'd seen in the last twenty-four hours, would take some getting used to.

CHAPTER 18

AT TEN PAST MIDNIGHT, THE Uber driver pulled into the parking lot of BJ's Buffalo Style Hot Wings next to the Graceland. Elvis exited the back of the car and slowly walked over to the place that had once been his home.

Victoria stayed in the Explorer with the driver.

In front of the mansion, Elvis leaned against the stonewall and looked through the spaces between the wrought iron fence poles. Up on the hill, he saw the mansion lit up and shining in the darkness.

Graceland always looked so peaceful this time of night.

When he first bought it, the mansion had been located outside the city limits. That hadn't stopped his fans from coming out here. That was why the fence now existed. Once it had been erected, countless girls came and wrote their numbers on its stones, hoping Elvis might give them a call.

He noticed all of the stones were covered with writings from fans over the many years, apparently including the four decades since he'd been…dead.

The house appeared much like it had for the last twenty years of his life. But it wasn't a home now. It was something else. And whatever that might be, it certainly wasn't his home anymore.

Yet the one constant that remained were his fans.

Even now, forty years after his grave said he'd died, his fans still came here. They hadn't forgotten him. How could that be? He hadn't done anything that memorable, had he?

Off to his right, about thirty feet away, he saw a young couple in their early twenties writing on his wall. Elvis walked over to them. "Excuse me," he said.

The young man looked at Elvis with some suspicion.

"I was just wondering, what are you writing there?" Elvis asked.

"We're leaving a message for Elvis," the young woman answered.

Elvis didn't understand this. "Uh…isn't Elvis dead?"

"Of course not," the young man said. "The King can never die."

This added to Elvis's confusion. "You mean I didn't…I mean, he didn't die in August of '77?"

"Oh, no, I'm not saying he faked his death," the young man said. His words shocked Elvis, but he did his best to hide it. "I mean Elvis's spirit will always live on."

"You know, you kinda look like him," the young woman said.

Finally, someone recognized him. Elvis allowed himself a smile. "Yeah. I've heard that a time or two in my life."

The young man looked Elvis up and down. "Yeah, you've got his eyes and his face. Plus, you sound a lot like him. If you dyed your hair, you could really pull off Big Elvis."

"Big Elvis?" What the heck was this fellow talking about?

"Tommy," the young woman said to her boyfriend, a touch of scorn in her voice.

"Sorry," Tommy said to Elvis. "That was a real jerk thing to say."

"It's all right, but what did you mean by it?" Elvis asked.

The woman answered, "You know. In his later years, Elvis didn't really take good care of himself."

"Yeah," Tommy said. "He got pretty heavy."

Elvis wanted to tell them off, but he knew they were right. He looked down at his stomach. It protruded out well past his waistline. He couldn't even see his toes. He didn't remember the last time he'd touched them.

"Thank you very much for your time," Elvis said, and turned back for the car.

"You really do sound a lot like him," the young woman said.

"Have a good one," Tommy added.

Elvis turned back to them. "Can I ask you one more thing?"

"Sure," the young woman said.

"How old are you two?"

"Twenty-five," Tommy said.

"Twenty-three," the woman said.

This didn't make any sense. They couldn't have seen him live or heard any of his songs on the radio. Elvis had to follow up on this. "If you were both born after I—after he died, why are you here?"

"Are you kidding me?" the woman said. "Elvis was the King of Rock and Roll. No one's ever topped that."

Wow, Elvis thought, then asked, "No one? Not even The Beatles?"

"They only built on what Elvis did," she said.

Elvis grinned. He'd outlasted The Beatles.

"And Elvis is far better than these crap singers they're forcing on us now," Tommy said. "He was the real deal. He had it, you know."

CHAPTER 19

BESIDES TELLING VICTORIA HE WANTED to go back to the hotel, Elvis didn't say anything else after climbing into the back of the Explorer. He stared out the window, watching everything pass by in the night. He didn't understand all that had happened to him, but one thing was clear: he'd messed up his life in a pretty big way.

Things hadn't worked out with Priscilla the way he'd wanted them to. He'd messed up badly with her. He didn't stand up to the Colonel when he should have. Despite the millions he'd been paid, those movies had turned him into a joke. Fortunately, the TV special and the concerts had saved his career. But that had gone wrong too.

That was a big reason he'd increased the amount of pills he'd been taking. If he hadn't hated the almost nonstop touring schedule, he probably wouldn't have taken so many. Maybe that wasn't true. He didn't know. But it had cost him everything, including his own life, it now seemed.

And what about his daughter? What had happened to little Lisa Marie? How had his death affected her? Being Elvis's daughter would bring its own unique set of issues, but would growing up without a father impact her life in even worse ways? He didn't even want to think about these things.

As they climbed out of the back of the vehicle at the Peabody, Victoria pulled him out of his thoughts.

"How are you doing?" she asked.

"If you woke up to find out that you ain't who you think you are and, on top of that, you've been dead for forty years, how would you be doing?"

"I think I'd be a bit messed up."

"That's one way of putting it, doc." Elvis felt lonelier than he'd felt in years. "Everything I had…everything I was…it's all gone."

"No, not all of it. You're right here now. That's got to count as something."

"But from what I worked out, in about two months, I'm gonna wind up dead."

"Who says it has to be that way?" Victoria asked.

"That tombstone over at my house made it pretty darned clear," Elvis said. "Heck, I didn't even live to see my fiftieth birthday."

"That fate doesn't have to be yours this time," Victoria said.

"I don't know. I've made so many mistakes."

Victoria touched his hand. He looked at her. She reminded him so much of Priscilla. But she wasn't. Priscilla had given up on him at a certain point, but this lady was still standing here with him.

"No one's ever had a second chance to get things right before, but you do," she said. "You have the opportunity to change the way your story ends. You can make better choices and you can make a huge difference in the world, and not just from your singing. Your being here could really take the paranoia and the stigma off human cloning."

"You saying that cloning's looked down on?" Elvis asked.

"Most people have a hard time separating science fiction from science fact."

"Then I guess there ain't too many clones like me walking around."

"You're actually the only one. You're unique."

Elvis took it all in. They'd always said he was unique. Even his mama had told him so. But that wasn't entirely true.

"Did you know I had a twin brother when I was born?"

"I did read that when I was getting up to date with you."

"Yeah. His name was Jesse. He was stillborn. I was born about a half-hour later. Mama used to tell me that God took him and spared me because I was special and he had a plan for me. Maybe he still does and that's why you cloned me. What do you think?"

"It doesn't really matter what I think. It only matters what you think."

Elvis nodded. She was right. Too many times he'd done what other people had told him to do or what they expected him to do, especially the Colonel. Elvis often didn't do what he really wanted to or thought he should. He hadn't had much control over anything since back when he was playing with Scotty and Bill and recording for Mr. Phillips.

That was how his life got out of control. He'd remained quiet and passive, even as things were eating him up on the inside. If he'd spoken up, if he'd expressed his own opinions, if he'd just said no, how different would things have turned out? Would he still be living at Graceland rather than buried there? Or would he simply have walked away from it all and found the nice, quiet life that had eluded him since his first appearance on *Louisiana Hayride*?

Maybe things would be different.

Or maybe none of it mattered.

But unlike other people, he was being given a second bite at the apple because they'd cloned him.

"You want to know what I think, doc?" Elvis said. "I don't think God makes mistakes, it's us people who do. And I think my mama was right. He did have a plan for me then, and I messed things up a bit. But somehow, I'm still here, which means he still has one for me. And if that's the case, then I definitely want to get things right this time."

CHAPTER 20

CAMERON OGILVIE COULDN'T REMEMBER THE last time he'd been this happy. Maybe when he'd made his first five hundred million?

He and Fatu met Victoria and Elvis in the lobby of the Peabody when they walked through the doors. The four took seats in the far corner of the lobby. Victoria explained to Cameron what had gone on and that Elvis wanted a second chance at life.

Seeing the clone had indeed changed his attitude, Cameron immediately dropped his. He apologized to Elvis for the things he said while frustrated. Elvis forgave him and they buried the hatchet.

"This is going to be great!" Cameron said. "Elvis...shoot, I probably shouldn't call you by your name until we're ready to unveil you to the world."

"Why don't you call me John?" Elvis said.

"That's right," Cameron said. "John Burrows. Your secret identity."

Cameron could see the surprise on Elvis's face when he mentioned the name. "How'd you know about that?"

"When I decided to clone you, I figured I better know everything there is to know about you, so I read and watched everything I could get my hands on the last few years."

"And people know about John Burrows?" Elvis asked.

"It's common knowledge," Cameron said. "Some of your

more intense fans even theorize about you still being alive and living in Kalamazoo, Michigan under that alias."

Again, Cameron could read the unexpected shock on the clone's face. It shouldn't have surprised Elvis that a portion of his fan base would not accept that he had really died in 1977. Plenty of people had exploited those fans' attachment to Elvis by selling them books and movies allegedly revealing that the King was still alive.

The amount those charlatans had made would be a rounding error compared to the hundreds of millions of dollars—if not billions—Cameron was poised to make now with his clone of Elvis Presley!

"All of your fans will go nuts when you hit the scene again," Cameron said. "Hell, the whole world is going to flip. You're going to be the biggest thing to happen to music since…well, since the last time you happened to music!"

"That's great, Mr. Ogilvie," Elvis said. "But before we get rolling, I got three conditions I'm gonna need you to meet."

"And what might those be?" Cameron asked, trying to hide his contempt. He could not stand performers who wanted to place conditions on his plans. They never seemed to realize he was the brains of the operation.

But he still needed a signed contract with the resurrected Elvis. He wasn't in a position to put his foot down, so he indulged the clone.

"First," Elvis said, "I don't wanna do any movies where I have to sing."

"No movies where you have to sing. That's fair to me. What else?"

"I want to pick my own songs. A lot of those that the Colonel had me doing were nothing but crap."

"Agreed. I would never want you singing a song that doesn't fit your brand."

"My brand?"

"Yes. All of the songs you record need to be Elvis-worthy. Which also requires that you trust me as well when it comes to musical selections. I don't want you singing anything that doesn't fit you and what we're trying to accomplish."

Elvis nodded. "I'm good with that."

"And what's your third condition?" Cameron asked.

"Well, the last time I was in Europe was back when I was in the Army. The Colonel always said we'd go there on tour, but we never did."

"Now if what you're asking me is if you'll have concert dates in Europe, you will. And not just there. I think you should tour the whole world this time around. How's that sound to you, *John*?"

Elvis smiled. "Like you're the kind of man who's good at taking care of business in a flash."

"You can bet your sideburns on that," Cameron said, and offered his hand.

Elvis shook it, cementing their deal.

PART III

GOT A LOT OF LIVIN' TO DO

CHAPTER 21

BY MIDMORNING, THEY WERE BACK on Cameron's jet flying west to Los Angeles. Once the plane had taken off, Elvis fell into a deep slumber. Two minutes after going to sleep, he started snoring loudly.

"Please tell me he's going to be all right," Cameron said to Victoria as he looked down at the snoring clone. Victoria came to stand next to him. She silently observed Elvis before responding.

"He's been taking pills to help him go to sleep and then to get up since who knows when," she said. "His system's going to need to adjust to not having them. He's probably going to sleep a lot."

"I get that, but once everything's out of his system, you're going to have to get him clean and keep him sober."

"Me?" Victoria asked. "I'm not a psychiatrist."

"But you are a doctor. And you know we can't take him to a regular shrink."

"No. I'm not doing that."

Cameron turned his attention directly to Victoria. "If he keels over and dies again, there's no way I'm going to be able to recoup the funds I spent cloning him. And without those funds, I won't have the ability to invest in the rest of your work."

Victoria glared at him. She should have known he'd try to change things on her.

"That wasn't our deal."

"Before you get your feathers in an uproar, think about this," Cameron said. "If he dies from an overdose again, do you think anyone's going to believe it was his fault? No. They'll say your cloning process is defective. You'll lose all credibility. We've got to get him cleaned up and ready to rock again."

"And by *we*, you're putting it all on me."

"No, we are one hundred percent in this together. I'm going to bring him up to speed on the four decades he's missed and all the music that's come out to get him ready to record. All I'm asking you to do is get him off the drugs and living healthy."

"Oh, I'm glad that's *all*."

"That's only half the task." Cameron pointed to Fatu sitting in a seat in the very rear of the cabin. "Fathead's going to have a bigger challenge getting him into a fitness routine and working all this blubber off."

If Fatu understood his role or felt slighted at the insult, his consistently stoic expression didn't reveal it.

"Victoria, don't you see? We've got to see this all the way through to getting him back on stage, or else everything will be for naught."

He was right, and she hated that. She also hated that she'd allowed him to manipulate the situation. She should have expected it, given their history. But Victoria knew the only person to blame was her. Cameron's stripes never changed. She'd allowed herself to momentarily ignore this, as his idea, as crazy as it may have been, was the fastest way to continue her work and reach her goal.

She reminded herself of this now. Her final goal. That was the only reason she'd agreed to clone Elvis. And that was why she would play her part to help put the risen icon back in the spotlight for Cameron.

CHAPTER 22

CAMERON MOVED ELVIS INTO THE guesthouse of his Brentwood mansion. The guesthouse's size impressed Elvis. It had a living room, a kitchen with a small dining room, two bedrooms, and two bathrooms. It was larger than the house he'd bought for his parents after making real money for the first time in his life.

The giant television suspended to the wall in the living room caught Elvis's attention.

"Holy macaroni," he said. "Now that there's a TV."

Cameron turned it on with a remote. The picture was incredibly clear and had great detail. Elvis had never seen anything like it. The images were better than anything he'd ever seen, even on the big screen at the cinema.

"You've got five hundred channels at your fingertips right here," Cameron said.

"Five hundred channels? How am I gonna have time to watch them all?" Elvis asked.

"You won't. Most people stick to the same five, if that. A lot of them have, as we say these days, 'cut the cord' and are primarily watching Netflix, Hulu, and Amazon."

"Like the rain forest in Latin America?"

"Yes, but useful and profitable."

Immediately, Elvis wanted to know about music. At his core, Elvis loved music as much as life. He wanted to hear and experience it in all of its forms and types. He had great curiosity about who and what had come about in his absence. He wanted to know about the changes. There was no way things could have stayed the same musically since '77. That was impossible.

Music always changed and evolved. It had changed dramatically in his lifetime, and not just with him and others bringing rock and roll to America and the world at large. All of the others who followed him changed music too. The changes that must have taken place during his forty-year absence excited him to some degree. They also frightened him. Despite what he'd heard from the young couple out front of Graceland, Elvis feared becoming irrelevant in the twenty-first century.

Cameron said he'd tutor Elvis on all the music he'd missed out on without delay. He asked Fatu to bring him something he called a "laptop." The Islander left and a few minutes later returned carrying a slender silver box in one hand.

Cameron took it from him, set it on the kitchen table, and pulled it apart in the middle, revealing a typewriter on the bottom half and a small TV screen on the other half.

"What the heck is this?" Elvis asked. "A TV built into a typewriter?"

"Actually, it's a computer," Cameron said.

"That's a dang computer?"

"Practically anything with electronics today is a computer. You'll be amazed at the things that are available with a few taps of your fingertips."

Elvis tried to wrap his brain around that. The future wasn't what he thought it would be, but man, it was still pretty wild.

"I reckon, then, that we're not heading out to the record store for you to bring me up to speed?" Elvis said.

Cameron smirked. "You reckon right. We're already at

the record store."

It took Elvis a moment, then he pointed a questioning finger at the laptop.

Tapping a few keys, Cameron opened something on the screen that he said was "iTunes." He then proceeded to explain to Elvis how records had gone out of style, being replaced partially by cassettes, then fully by compact discs, which were then eliminated by digital music thanks to Steve Jobs and his iPod.

"So nobody buys records anymore?" Elvis asked.

"Actually, vinyl has made a significant comeback, especially with collectors and purists. But for the most part, people download their music."

He clicked a couple buttons, then typed in *Elvis Presley*.

"Your entire catalogue is available right here," Cameron said.

Elvis couldn't believe it. The titles of all the songs he'd recorded both in the studio and in concert were displayed there on the screen.

Cameron pointed to a record cover that Elvis didn't recognize. "There's even a few new versions of your older songs."

Cameron clicked the remixed version of "A Little Less Conversation."

Elvis listened to twenty seconds of the song, then said, "That ain't bad."

"It was a pretty big hit. You also might enjoy this."

Cameron took him next to an album titled *If I Can Dream*. He clicked on "Burning Love." It wasn't the song Elvis remembered. While it still featured his vocals, the band had been replaced with an orchestra.

"What do you think?" Cameron asked.

"It's good, but it don't sound quite right without my band backing me."

"Without any new recordings, people have become desperate. It's not like you're Prince with a vault."

"Prince who?" Elvis asked.

Cameron smiled. "Why don't we start with 1977 and move forward from there."

CHAPTER 23

CAMERON STARTED HIS MUSICAL TUTORIAL with the Bee Gees and that disco trend that had been growing in popularity at the time of his death. Elvis enjoyed the Bee Gees, in particular the song "Staying Alive."

"Guess that's kind of your theme song right now," Cameron said.

"Indeed it is."

As the 1970s ended and rolled into the 1980s, rock took a bit of a different turn. Not worse, just different. New wave didn't much appeal to Elvis, but Michael Jackson impressed him.

"Little Michael Jackson's really come a long way," Elvis said.

"Well, for a while, he was your son-in-law," Cameron said.

"He was my what?" Elvis wasn't sure he'd heard right.

"We'll talk about that later. Let me introduce you to Prince."

Cameron started with the album *1999* and went into *Purple Rain*. Elvis liked Prince a lot. The lyrics of his songs were magical.

"Man, this guy's really something," Elvis said.

"Yeah, he sure was."

"Was?"

"Let's just say you're not the only musical icon to die an

untimely death."

Cameron next brought up *Appetite for Destruction.* The music of Guns N' Roses did not impress Elvis one bit.

"That boy sounds like he's wrassling with a gator," he said, shaking his head at the vocal stylings of Axl Rose.

"He has one of the most distinct voices in rock and roll."

"No," Elvis said. "Jackie Wilson and Roy Orbison. Those are distinct voices. This boy's just screaming and hollering like some kind of maniac."

"Well, listen to this."

Cameron clicked on "Sweet Child o' Mine."

Elvis listened until the first chorus. "That one's not too bad. The fella who's playing that guitar could give Scotty a run for his money, but I don't get what anyone would see in this singer, man. What the heck happened to rock and roll?"

"A lot of it went over country."

Cameron found Hank Williams Jr. and cued up "All My Rowdy Friends Are Coming Over Tonight." Elvis bopped his head along with the beat.

"We used to listen to his daddy all time when I was growing up," Elvis said. "Now Junior here, this boy can sing."

Together they listened to the greatest hits of the last forty years. Sadly, the music of the last decade disappointed and started to depress Elvis. The filthy language and the lack of instruments being played undermined what he considered music. He found solace, however, in country music, particularly Garth Brooks and Taylor Swift, even though this wasn't the kind of country music his parents had raised him on.

Garth Brooks made a powerful impact on Elvis. "Now here's a singer," he said.

"Some people consider him to be the Elvis of country music," Cameron said.

"Ain't nobody ever gonna be better than Hank Williams."

"Garth's record sales might argue with you on that point."

Elvis listened to all of Garth's songs. He had Cameron play "The Dance" twice for him. The song spoke deeply to his soul. It haunted him. He could relate to its lyrics on a deeply personal level. He had been the King, or so people liked to say. But there was so much he would have done differently if he knew then what he did now.

As he'd expected, music had changed greatly in his absence. Yep, music always had and always would change. He'd played a major role in part of its transformation, bringing hillbilly songs and black music together, helping to launch what would be rock and roll. It had changed during his career, first with surf music, then the British invasion, and with the hard rock sounds that followed.

Elvis had adapted and survived too. Barely at times, but still, he'd made it when others had thought him down for the count. But could he evolve and make a comeback now? Did 2017 have a place for Elvis Presley?

CHAPTER 24

"WHAT THE HECK IS THIS?" Elvis asked Victoria as he put a dinner plate full of foods he had never seen before in front of him at the dining room table.

"It's your dinner," she said, pointing to the different foods she was serving. "Quinoa, carrots, and Brussels sprouts."

"But where's the meat?"

"This is a vegan dish."

"Don't you be trying to get me to turn vegetarian, doc—"

"A vegan diet is a little more than vegetarian. Or, actually, it's a bit less, as there's zero dairy and zero honey in it."

Elvis pushed the plate away. "Look, I know you're trying to help, but I just can't eat this stuff."

"Not to be morbid over dinner, but if you want to avoid a heart attack in about two months, you'll need to learn to do so."

"I thought y'all said it was the pills that caused it?" Elvis asked.

"I've reviewed all the records available about your death," she said, hesitating after saying the word. "The pills definitely played a part in it, but you still had a heart attack at the age of forty-two. That didn't come about by the pills alone. You had—actually still have—heart disease. And the only way you can reverse that and heal your heart is to go on a plant-based diet."

Victoria moved the plate back in front of him.

"You saying I can't have any more cheeseburgers?" Elvis asked.

"Not if you want to live to see your fiftieth birthday."

Elvis thought about it and shook his head. "I can't see how never having a cheeseburger is any type of living anyone would want to do."

"I'll make a deal with you," Victoria said. "If you get down to one hundred and eighty-five pounds and maintain it for a month, you can have a cheat day every other week."

"A cheat day?" Elvis asked, intrigued.

"One day every two weeks when you can eat what you want to. Cheeseburger, french fries, donuts, whatever you want."

Elvis knew exactly what he wanted. "A grilled banana and peanut butter sandwich?" he asked, starting to salivate as he imagined it.

Victoria grimaced. "If that's what you want."

"Don't knock it till you try it, doc."

"Fair enough. But first, you've got to lose the weight."

Elvis gave in and picked up his fork. "All right. You got yourself a deal, doc."

Victoria smiled and Elvis harpooned a Brussels sprout with his fork and put it his mouth. A second later, his face revealed his disgust at the food.

"Ugh," he said. "This tastes horrible."

"Your taste buds simply aren't used to good, natural, healthy food."

Elvis forked a couple of carrots into his mouth. He chewed then asked with his mouth full, "Can I at least put some butter and salt on this stuff?"

Victoria shook her head. "Sorry. But don't worry, keep eating these foods and you'll come to enjoy all of them."

"Don't count on it, doc," Elvis said as he prepared to eat quinoa for the first time in his life.

CHAPTER 25

AFTER VICTORIA LEFT, ELVIS SETTLED onto the sofa with a Diet Coke and some rice cake snacks she said he could eat if he got hungry. It was time for him to catch up on things with this so-called "smart TV" Cameron had explained to him.

Elvis launched the Netflix program thingamajig and brought up the CNN show *The Seventies*. He stayed up all night watching every episode. The next two nights, he binged *The Eighties* and *The Nineties*.

Ronald Reagan becoming president shocked Elvis. He knew Reagan had been governor of California and had tried to run against Jerry Ford in '76, but Elvis couldn't see the country electing Reagan. His movie career hadn't been much better than Elvis's. And at least Elvis never had a chimp as a costar.

Elvis cheered seeing the footage of the Berlin Wall finally coming down. He took pride in playing a small part in standing up to those dang Russians as a solider stationed in West Germany during the Cold War. It made him think about Priscilla and how they'd met. If he hadn't been drafted and sent off to Germany, they never would have met. They never would have married and they never would have had Lisa Marie.

Elvis didn't want to think about that, so he went searching for things on more recent history. He didn't like what he discovered.

While the twentieth century had ended on a high note for the United States, the twenty-first century started with incredible tragedy.

He watched a documentary on September 11, 2001 and cried when the Twin Towers came down. It made him feel angry, but also vulnerable. Vulnerable was exactly how he'd felt since waking up.

That feeling continued to grip him. He didn't like being unarmed and that he couldn't get any guns. You never knew who was out there. Now with these terrorist killers, Elvis wanted to be prepared if he ran into them. He didn't like not having any guns.

Elvis shut off the giant TV and went into the kitchen. Still sitting at the table was Cameron's laptop. Elvis opened it and sat down. Cameron had told him that this Google doohickey could tell him anything and everything he'd ever want to ask or know. All he had to do was type in the subject or question he had then press the button marked "return."

He'd never learned to type. When Elvis had grown up, women learned to type to become secretaries. Men learned how to build things and drive trucks to support themselves and their families. That was what he'd done, become a truck driver. He wondered if that was the way it still was or if everyone had to learn how to type, given the abundance of computers in the world.

Carefully, using his two index fingers and watching the typewriter letters closely, Elvis typed two words into the allegedly all-knowing Google contraption, his daddy's name, Vernon Presley.

He read about his daddy dying in 1979. He cried, mourning the loss of his father. After letting it all out, he felt relief that Daddy and Mama were finally together again in heaven. She probably gave him heck for remarrying so fast, but she'd forgive him. She always had. She loved him.

Next, Elvis looked for information about his Minnie Mae Presley, whom he affectionately called Dodger, and his aunt, Delta Presley Biggs.

Dodger went to heaven the year after Daddy died. Aunt Delta survived them all, making it all the way to 1993. Must've been her meanness that scared death off her doorstep a time or two.

Elvis smiled remembering all of the times he'd thought of Delta when performing "Polk Salad Annie." The image of her in his mind always helped him put more into that song and bring it to life for his audiences.

Next, Elvis pecked in the name of Colonel Tom Parker.

The Colonel had passed in 1990. This elicited a strange sadness in Elvis. For the last several years, he'd grown to resent his manager, especially because of all the touring and the twice-nightly shows in Las Vegas.

But if it hadn't been for the Colonel, Elvis knew he never would have made it like he had. He never would have become as rich as he had and he never would have bought Graceland for his parents. The Colonel had taken him to RCA and put him on television. That was when Elvis went national and everything changed.

Elvis got angry when he finally learned the reason why the Colonel had never let him tour in Europe or any place outside the United States. The Colonel had been here illegally. He couldn't have left America without risking that he wouldn't be let back into the country.

The Colonel's name wasn't even Tom Parker. It was Andreas Cornelius van Kujik. How he got the name Tom Parker out of that, Elvis didn't have a clue. He let the matter go, knowing he'd now be able to tour internationally this time under Mr. Ogilvie's management.

Elvis wondered about what had become of his closest friends and his entourage. The information he found shouldn't have surprised him, given the time that had passed, but it did break his heart.

Joe Esposito, Lamar Fike, Charlie Hodge, and Sam Phillips—they were all gone.

It seemed that nearly everyone he'd been close to in his life were all dead.

He wondered about Hank Miceli. Hank used to live here in LA. He'd been younger than the rest of them by a good ten years or so. Maybe he still lived here.

Elvis pecked in the name and city. He found a Henry Miceli, age seventy-eight, living in an apartment in Santa Monica. That had to be *Henri*, as Elvis used to call him.

Elvis considered calling Hank up, but there wasn't a phone number listed with the address. That would probably be for the best. Such a call would open up a whole can of fishing worms. Besides, how could he really explain that he'd been cloned and all that?

Finally, it was time for him to look up the person he wanted to find out about the most. He'd put it off, fearful of what he might find. But now, seeing that so many people he cared for had died over the last forty years, he didn't see any good reason to put it off any longer.

Elvis used his two fingers to type in the name that meant more to him than all the others he'd asked about on Google.

Priscilla Presley.

CHAPTER 26

THREE SECONDS AFTER TYPING HER name into Google, pictures of his Priscilla came up, and written information with things Cameron had called "links" attached to each one.

Elvis exhaled.

After all this time, after all these years, after all they'd been through, Priscilla still took his breath away. Elvis started reading the information Google had on her.

Priscilla was seventy-two now and still looked incredible. She wasn't the innocent, beautiful young thing he'd first met in Bad Nauheim, but she still did it for him. It was odd. Elvis had always been older than her. Now, she was thirty years older than him.

She'd gone on to become an actress. Some movie called *The Naked Gun* seemed to be her most talked about picture. He'd have to see if he could watch that on Netflix or Rain Forest or some other station.

Next, Elvis went back to the Google starting point and tapped in another name close to his heart.

Lisa Marie Presley.

Google showed Elvis something that shocked him, though he should have been aware of it, given the passage of time. His little girl wasn't a little girl anymore. In fact, like her mother, Lisa Marie was now older than him. She was forty-nine and had grown into a beautiful woman. Still, Elvis could see there was something sullen about her face in all the pictures he found of her.

How had his death affected her? Had it complicated her life in ways he couldn't have considered? Being his daughter, he knew she'd never have a life that most people would consider *normal*, but had his absence from her life made things worse?

Elvis never liked to dwell on regrets. Bad things happened in his life. That was just the way things worked in this world. He'd lived a life that was blessed a million times over. He pushed his mind to focus on brighter thoughts. He'd definitely done some things wrong in the past, but now he had a new future before him. He was committed to doing things right.

A photo of Lisa Marie with four other people of various ages caught his attention. Elvis clicked on it to learn that his little girl now had four kids of her own.

Whoa! Those four children were his grandkids.

He laughed at the thought of himself, Elvis Presley, being a grandfather. Who'd believe that? Heck, who'd believe he was alive again as a ditto of himself?

Ditto or not, he was a granddad—their granddad. He'd buy them all horses and go riding. They'd have cookouts and sing songs. It would be the best kind of fun.

CHAPTER 27

CAMERON SAT DOWN FOR BREAKFAST with his attorney Skylar Kauffman on the outside patio behind his Brentwood mansion.

"Cameron, I love you like a son, but what you're asking me to put in this contract is highly illegal," Skylar said.

"I don't see it that way," Cameron said, buttering one side of an English muffin.

"What you're asking him to sign could be defined as violating the Thirteenth Amendment."

"*Could* be."

"Could *easily* be."

"That's still an equivocation on your part." Cameron sank his teeth into the muffin.

"Under the bizarre circumstances here, you might be able to persuade a judge, but why take the risk?"

"Because risking's what I do," Cameron said as he chewed. "You of all people should know that by now."

"Even so, you'll never get him to sign this."

"Have you ever seen some of the contracts Elvis signed?" Cameron asked as he poured himself a second cup of coffee. "Tom Parker took him to the cleaners for over twenty years, and all Elvis ever said was, 'Thank you, thank you very much.'"

The conversation stopped as the door from the house opened and Elvis came outside to join them.

"The man of the hour," Cameron said. "We were just talking about you. Elvis, I'd like you to meet the world's best entertainment lawyer, Skylar Kauffman."

Skylar stood up. Elvis offered his hand to the silver-haired lawyer.

"Pleased to meet you, Mr. Kauffman."

"The pleasure is all mine, Mr. Presley, I've been a been a big fan all of my life."

"Thank you, Mr. Kauffman. But call me Elvis. That's my name."

Skylar returned to his seat. Elvis took the open chair across from Cameron.

Cameron said, "I asked Sky to join us so we could all talk over some business particulars."

"That's great," Elvis said, "But before we do that, Mr. Ogilvie, there's some people I'd like to meet."

Cameron hadn't seen this coming. "And who's that?" he asked, trying to keep the concern out of his voice.

"Well, Riley and Benjamin and Finley and Harper."

Cameron had no clue what Elvis was talking about. "I'm not familiar with those names," Cameron said. "Are they musicians you discovered?"

"No, sir," Elvis said. "They're my grandkids."

"Your grandkids?" Cameron said.

"Yes, sir. I learned about them from the Google machine last night. Lisa Marie's got four kids, if you can believe that. And I'd really like to meet them."

This wasn't good. Cameron couldn't let such an unorthodox reunion happen. It could jeopardize everything he was doing. But he couldn't risk shooting the clone's request down directly, either.

"That's very understandable," Cameron said. "But we should wait until after we announce your return."

"But I really don't want to wait to meet 'em."

"Elvis," Cameron said, "back in Memphis, we agreed to keep things on the down-low until after we reveal your existence to the world."

"I know, but that's with the general public," Elvis said. "This is family we're talking about."

"Yes, but none of them know you're alive."

"I know." Elvis chuckled. "Heck, none of them were born before I kicked the old bucket."

"And it could be a bit of a shock to have their grandfather who's never been around at all to suddenly show up in their lives."

"Well, I figure you and the doc could explain this whole cloning thing to them just like you did for me," Elvis said.

Cameron didn't know what to do. He needed Elvis happy and working toward his comeback. He didn't need any interference from the Presley family. Most importantly, he needed Elvis to sign the damn contract. That meant there was only one thing to do.

He needed to buy time by lying and manipulating his dimwitted clone.

"You're right," Cameron said. "There's no reason your family shouldn't know about your revival. But let's think about the best way to handle this. I think we should still wait until we reveal your return to the public. That way, when your grandkids see you, you'll be fit and ready to rock. I think that's the man you'd most want them to see, isn't it?

"I do, but—"

"Perfect," Cameron said. "I'll have Sky track them all down and we'll invite them out here right after the announcement of your return. How's that sound?"

"Well," Elvis said, "maybe that is best."

"Trust me," Cameron said. "It absolutely is."

Elvis nodded his agreement. "Thank you, Mr. Ogilvie. I really do appreciate it."

"And I appreciate you and all you're doing, Elvis," Cameron said. "You've already lost weight, haven't you?"

"Eleven pounds so far," Elvis said with a touch of pride.

"It shows, and you're looking good," Cameron said. "Now, Sky and I were discussing how, before we get too far down the road, you and I should make sure our entire arrangement is both proper and official, to protect both of our interests. You know what I'm saying?"

"Absolutely, Mr. Ogilvie," Elvis said. "Just let me know what we need to do."

That was exactly what Cameron wanted to hear. He looked at Skylar. Skylar looked back. He obviously remained hesitant about this. Cameron hardened his stare. Skylar gave in and passed the contract over to Elvis.

As Elvis picked it up, Cameron casually slid his personalized gold pen across the table to the clone. Elvis picked it up and, without reading a single word of the contract, flipped to the last page, where he signed his name.

Cameron shared a sly smile with Sky and said, "Well, it's all official now. The King is coming back."

CHAPTER 28

ANOTHER STEP THAT WENT ALONG with giving up the pills and eating so-called real food was exercising. Changing his diet wouldn't be enough for Elvis to lose the excess poundage he carried. He needed a solid cardio and resistance training to regain his physical prowess.

A large room in Cameron Ogilvie's mansion served as a gymnasium.

Fatu had Elvis lifting weights on Monday, Wednesday, and Friday, and doing cardio on Tuesdays, Thursdays, and Saturdays. Sundays were the only day Elvis wasn't required to work out.

The normally silent Fatu actually spoke during the workouts, but seldom more than two words: "More" and "Again." Other than that, he simply pointed and directed Elvis to the different weight machines.

The first week had been rough. The upper body strength Elvis once had, especially when he served in the Army, no longer existed. He needed to rebuild his muscles. Being overweight didn't help.

But after a week and a half, Elvis noticed his strength increasing. He could see muscle tone returning to his arms and legs. The grueling workout schedule Fatu had created was producing results.

A month into things, Elvis decided to incorporate his previous martial arts routine into his training.

"You know karate?" Elvis asked Fatu.

"Judo," Fatu responded.

It made sense. Being built like a small boulder, judo would appeal more to Fatu, as it involved more grappling and wrestling than karate. Part of Elvis's motivation in asking if the Islander knew karate was because he always enjoyed showing off his skills and training others. But with Fatu knowing judo, that presented its own challenge.

"You wanna spar?" Elvis asked.

Fatu responded not with words, but by breaking into a judo fighting stance. Elvis smiled. He always enjoyed sparring, especially with a seemingly unmovable foe like Fatu.

The two went at it for the next fifteen minutes. Elvis had speed and skills. Fatu had strength and stamina. They were evenly matched. Neither could overcome the other. Fatu's endurance finally bested Elvis. As Elvis tired, Fatu got a hold of him and threw the clone across the room.

That also happened to be the moment Cameron stepped into his gym.

"What the hell do you think you're doing?" he yelled.

Fatu looked at Cameron and didn't say a word. Elvis could see Cameron was about to blow his stack at the bodyguard turned personal trainer, and intervened.

"Don't be mad at him, Mr. Ogilvie," Elvis said. "I'm the one who asked him to spar."

"To spar? Are you crazy? I didn't bring you back so you could break your neck pretending you're Jackie Chan."

"Who?" Elvis asked.

"Never mind. Lift weights, jog on the treadmill, sweat to the oldies, but no more sparring," Cameron said. Then he turned to Fatu. "I don't care what he says—if I catch you doing something like that again, you're going to be out on your ass, fathead."

Cameron stormed out of the gym.

Elvis looked over to Fatu.
“Sorry ’bout that,” Elvis said.
Fatu responded with a grunt.

CHAPTER 29

"HOW ARE YOU FEELING?" VICTORIA asked Elvis as they sat down on the living room sofa in the guesthouse.

"All right, I guess," Elvis said. "Just really tired."

"That's your body getting used to not relying on medication."

"Yeah, it's been so long since I wasn't taking anything that I really don't know how I'm supposed to feel."

"Do you remember when you started taking pills?" she asked.

Elvis went back in his mind to another time.

"Yeah," he said. "'Bout the time me and Scotty and Bill hit the road."

"And how long ago was that?"

"Twenty years or so, I guess."

Victoria quickly did the math in her head, adding in forty years to the clone's timeline. "So, 1957?"

"More like '55."

"Do you remember why you started taking the pills?"

Elvis shrugged. "Heck, everybody took 'em, mostly to stay awake on the road. Those were some long drives."

"But that wasn't the only time you took them?"

"No, I liked the energy they gave me. Especially when I went on stage. They really helped. I'd be so nervous."

"Is that when you started taking the sleeping pills too?" she asked.

"Well, yeah, just to balance things out," Elvis said, then added, "It made sense 'cause I always kept a pretty backward schedule."

Victoria nodded. Such was often the case with addicts. It started small and simple, then grew into something else. And then the addict found a rationalization for their behavior.

"And how do you feel now that you haven't been using them?"

"Horrible," Elvis said. He looked down at the carpet. He wouldn't look her in the eye. "And like a damned fool."

"Why's that?"

"Because I didn't mean for any of this to happen. I thought I had it all under control. I didn't think I was hooked. If I could do it all over again, I'd do it pretty different than I did."

"That's good."

Elvis finally looked at her again. "It is?"

"Yes," she said, and put her hand on his knee. "By admitting that, you've taken your first step to getting sober in your mind, not just in your body."

CHAPTER 30

NOT BEING ABLE TO LEAVE Cameron's home to go out and do things began to weigh on Elvis. He was accustomed to living separately from the world, but he'd never been this isolated. Rather than dwell on those thoughts, he focused on getting healthy, losing weight, and preparing to sing again. But he could only do so much of that.

The nights were the hardest time for him. The doc never stayed past nine. Cameron always went to bed by ten. Fatu kept late hours but wasn't much of a conversationalist.

Elvis hated being alone. And he hated sleeping alone. He wished Victoria would stay later, maybe even spend the night. But she was his doctor and he was pretty sure they had rules against things like that. Besides, he wasn't certain she was interested in him that way. He never made an advance on a woman unless he knew she'd accept it. The one thing Elvis hated more than being alone was rejection.

In his previous life, Elvis would have taken some Demerol to fall asleep. That always helped him. That was no longer an option for him. Not only did he want to stay clean and sober so he could stay alive, he didn't have any to take if he wanted to.

At first, Elvis would sit up and watch movies on sleepless nights. He'd watch the ones he'd loved and catch up on the ones he'd missed. There were plenty of both. Tonight, though, Elvis wasn't in the mood for any movies.

Wandering around the quiet guesthouse, he turned his attention to the computer sitting on the coffee table. That internet-thing-a-ma-bob presented him with unlimited possibilities to explore the world, even though he couldn't leave Cameron's property. He sat down and opened the laptop. What could he go searching for tonight?

Elvis looked at his fingers hovering over the typewriter keys. They looked so bare without rings. That's what he needed, some rings and some other jewelry. He'd been feeling naked without any. It was time to fix that. He might not be able to go to a real store, but he could go shopping through this computer. Shopping always lifted his spirits when he felt blue.

He pulled up the Amazon Rain Forest web page and typed in a search for men's jewelry. He found plenty of it. He saw lots of rings he liked and hit the orange "Add to Cart" button next to each one. Cameron had showed him how to do this when they were looking for records that weren't on the iTunes. He also told Elvis to purchase anything he wanted as Cameron's credit card was already on file with the website.

While Cameron hadn't specifically said to buy music only, Elvis didn't think ordering some jewelry would be out of line. Elvis always wore gold rings and necklaces. His fans would expect him to have them on when he went public. Cameron knew everything about Elvis's life. He had to know his love of gold accessories.

Elvis found a 14-karat gold necklace with a large cross attached to it. That would look good around his neck. He'd never been shy about his belief in Jesus. His mama would be proud of him wearing that too. He added it to the growing list of items in the invisible cart.

It dawned on Elvis that he should get something nice for Victoria too. A ring would be too much. A nice bracelet or necklace would be good. He could gauge her reaction and determine if she might be interested in him the way he was interested in her. If she wasn't, well, he could simply say he gave her the gift for bringing him back and giving him a second chance at life.

After nearly an hour of online shopping, Elvis still wasn't tired. He wondered about what else he might be able to buy through the computer. One of them portable phones might be a good thing. Cameron, Victoria, and even Fatu carried one with them at all times. He should have a phone too. Especially in case something bad happened to him.

While it turned out that he hadn't been abducted, Elvis knew there were plenty of whacky folks out there who would kidnap him and demand a ransom if they could. If he had a portable phone stashed away—a burner, as he'd heard it called in a couple movies—he could guard against that.

Yeah, having a burner phone was a good idea. But if he really wanted to fend off any kidnapping attempts, Elvis knew what he needed. He needed guns.

Unfortunately, he couldn't find any firearms in the Rain Forest. This didn't stop Elvis. He knew the Google machine could help him locate guns for sale, which it did. With a few pecks of his fingertips, Elvis found a giant sporting goods store with a huge listing of guns for sale.

Elvis ordered up a Smith & Wesson .38 special revolver and a 9mm Taurus pistol plus plenty of ammunition for both. But he didn't get much further than that. Before the store would allow him purchase his guns and ammo, its website required him to enter his personal information for some kind of a federal background check.

He couldn't enter his name, address, and date of birth into the boxes on the screen. Elvis was supposed to be dead, not living in the guesthouse of a record producer in Brentwood. On top of that, Elvis wasn't sure what birthday to type into the box. Was his birthday the day he first entered the world in 1935, or the day he woke up at Bio-Design in 2017?

Disappointed and confused, Elvis closed out of the sporting goods store website. Why would anyone need a background check to buy guns? Had the world gone crazy in the last forty years? The twenty-first century certainly had some drawbacks.

Maybe not.

Elvis had watched a documentary about something called "the dark web." There was allegedly all sorts of stuff found in that place that wasn't on the regular internet. Perhaps he could find a way to purchase some guns that way and not have to do one of those background checks.

CHAPTER 31

THE AMAZON DELIVERIES STARTED ARRIVING on Wednesday morning and didn't stop until Friday evening. Cameron stormed into the guesthouse, followed by Victoria. Elvis looked up from his spot on the sofa. He was trying on a diamond studded gold ring he'd removed from one of many boxes he was in the process of opening.

"What the hell do you think you're doing?" Cameron demanded.

Elvis shrugged. "I just needed to buy some things, Mr. Ogilvie."

"Some things? Do you know how stupid you've been?"

"Hey!" Elvis said, jumping to his feet. "No one calls me stupid." He didn't like the return of Cameron's mouthy side.

Victoria stepped forward. "Why don't you both calm down and discuss this rationally?"

"Rationally?" Cameron said. "Citi Bank just called me worried about my account being compromised because I'd made over twenty thousand dollars in online jewelry purchases this week."

"I was just picking up some stuff I needed," Elvis said, indicating the Amazon shipping boxes. "You know, before we go public with me being cloned and all."

"Purchases like this are reckless," Cameron said. "They send up red flags and get people asking questions who shouldn't be asking them. You can't risk our plans being ruined when we're so close to making the announcement."

"I understand that, Mr. Ogilvie, but I had to do something or I was gonna go crazy."

"Binge the new season of *Stranger Things*, then," Cameron said.

"I already did. And I've watched everything else I want to watch."

"Then just sit tight. It's only a matter of days now."

"You don't get it," Elvis said. "I'm feeling like a turkey, all cooped up, waiting to get his head lopped off for Thanksgiving dinner. I need to do something. Maybe even get out in the real world for a while."

"Out of the question," Cameron said.

"Maybe it's not a bad idea," Victoria said.

"It's a horrible idea," Cameron said. "All it takes is one person to spot him, take a video, tweet it to TMZ, and everything we've been working toward will be gone."

"But no one's looking for Elvis walking around," Victoria said.

"That's right," Elvis said. "And you haven't even let me dye my hair back to black yet. I could wear a hat, maybe even put on some blue jeans, if I had to."

"No," Cameron said. "We can't take the risk."

Elvis decided he'd press his case. With the doc on his side, maybe he could sway Cameron.

"Mr. Ogilvie, you have no idea what it's been like my entire adult life not being able to go out there and just be a normal person. As soon as we have this press conference, that's how it's going to be again."

"He's got a point, Cameron," Victoria said.

"This doesn't concern you," Cameron told her.

"Oh, I believe it does," she said. "You appointed me as his physician and his psychiatrist. I think a little field trip as a break from this place would do him some good."

"And it would really mean the world to me, Mr. Ogilvie," Elvis added.

Cameron took a deep breath and closed his eyes. Elvis couldn't tell if the producer's head was about to explode or if he was going to give in to the request. Elvis prepared himself for the explosion, but it didn't happen.

Cameron opened his eyes and exhaled everything in his lungs.

"Fine," Cameron said, "but I don't want you gone for more than three hours." He turned to Victoria. "And I don't want you to even think of leaving his side. Should anything go wrong, I'm holding you completely responsible."

"There's a surprise," Victoria said, then looked at Elvis. "Any idea where you want to go?"

CHAPTER 32

ELVIS WANTED TO SEE HOLLYWOOD. While he wasn't proud of the films he'd made, he'd always loved the movies. The allure of Tinseltown had never worn off for him. Hollywood Boulevard had changed a lot since he'd last been there. Amongst the people in costumes milling around outside of the historic Chinese Theater was a man in a white jumpsuit with gold sunglasses on his face and wearing a black pompadour wig.

"I'm not sure how I feel about all these fellas who get dressed up like me," Elvis said.

"Isn't imitation the sincerest form of flattery?" Victoria asked.

"I reckon you're right, but it's still a bit strange."

"There are a lot of Elvis impersonators. They more or less gave Cameron the idea to clone you in the first place."

"And that's how you got mixed up with him in all this, huh, doc?"

"You don't have to always call me doc."

"Well, you're my doctor. Just heard you say so to Mr. Ogilvie."

"Yes, but in social settings it's probably more appropriate for you to call me Victoria."

"Yeah, I guess I could, but it sounds a bit too formal. What's your middle name?"

"Lynn. But I've never been called that."

"Vicky Lynn." Elvis liked that. "How's that sound?"

"Sounds pretty Southern," she said.

"Well, I am Southern born and raised."

"You are indeed."

"So tell me, Vicky Lynn," Elvis said. "How'd you get mixed up with a guy like Cameron Ogilvie in the first place?"

"I don't think you want to know."

"Don't think I would've asked if I didn't."

Victoria took a moment before she answered. "It was through marriage, actually."

"Oh, so you're, like, cousins or something."

"No," she said. "He was my husband."

This halted Elvis in his tracks.

"Holy macaroni," he said. This could complicate things with her.

"Is it that hard to believe?" she asked.

"No, you're a very pretty lady. I can see why he'd come after you. But he don't really seem like he'd be your type."

Victoria started walking again. It took Elvis a couple of steps to catch up with her.

"Now he isn't," she said. "But back in college, when we met, he was different."

"I've definitely seen money change people and make them do some weird things. Some of the things I found on that internet say that's what happened to me."

"From what I know of you, you never lost your heart. Cameron, however…I'm not sure he still has one. But he always had money. That's not what happened to him."

"Then what was it?"

Elvis noticed his question made her flinch. He reached over and took her arm. They both stopped on the sidewalk. He turned her to face him and looked into her eyes. They were beautiful. All of her was beautiful. But she was sad. This conversation had done it.

"What's wrong?" he asked.

"I haven't talked about this in a long time," she said. Victoria lowered her face, not looking him in the eye as she spoke. "We were married about three years when I got pregnant. I had a little boy." She paused before saying the last part. "We lost him when he was three."

Each of her eyes shed a tear. He could see how deep the pain remained for her. He wondered if his mama had carried the same type of pain for Jesse throughout her life.

"I'm sorry, Vicky Lynn," Elvis said.

"It's not your fault. It's not really anyone's fault. But if you ever hear Cameron talk about it, which I'm sure you won't, he'll let you know that it was my fault."

"Then he's a damn fool."

"Not entirely," she said, wiping the tears off her cheeks. "But I don't really want to get more into this tonight. We're supposed to be out having a good time, right?"

"You're right, but so am I. He's a damn fool, especially for letting a woman like you go."

Elvis decided to take a chance. He lifted her chin with two fingers. Victoria looked up at him again. He stared deeply into her eyes, leaned in, and tenderly kissed her lips.

CHAPTER 33

TWO WEEKS LATER, CAMERON OGILVIE called for a press conference at his CEO Music offices, announcing the biggest news in music in a generation. Elvis had lost the weight and was in great shape. He'd worked hard and it had paid off. That day, he'd dyed his hair black for the first time since his return.

It was time to reveal the resurrected Elvis to the world.

The thought scared Elvis. He couldn't sleep at all the night before. Would everyone think it was all a joke? Had the world changed too much to want him? Would they even care that he was back? He'd faced these fears when he was drafted and when his movie career floundered. Both times, he'd been wrong. But he'd been gone for forty years. Making a comeback now might be too much to ask of his fans, many of whom were now dead themselves.

He thought about taking a couple of Demerol he'd bought online. While Cameron had made Elvis return everything he'd purchased from Amazon, he didn't know about the pills. Elvis had stashed them under his bed in case he needed them. So far, he hadn't, but tonight was different. Sleep would not come. He was nervous and on edge. Taking a couple would fix that. He'd get some sleep and be ready for tomorrow.

But he'd also let Vicky Lynn down. She'd worked with him to get clean, and had succeeded. He didn't want to betray the trust she had in him. Something more than a doctor-patient relationship was happening between them now. Elvis didn't want to blow that.

More importantly, he didn't want to blow the promise he'd made to himself in Memphis. Elvis wanted to do things differently this time. He wanted to do things right. And knowing the toll the pills had taken on him meant that taking them again would not be doing things the right way.

Instead of moving the mattress to retrieve the Demerol, Elvis got up, went into the living room, and popped on *Star Wars*. He loved the *Star Wars* movies, and that *Last Jedi* picture coming out in December would be his first chance to see one of them in a cinema.

When Cameron had first explained how he could watch any movie he wanted on the guesthouse's big-screen TV, Elvis told him he wanted to see *Star Wars*. He'd wanted to see it that night back in Missouri, but it wasn't showing there.

"Which one do you want to watch?" Cameron asked.

Elvis had had no idea there was more than one *Star Wars* movie. He'd learned there was indeed more than one movie—eight had been released, with more on the way for as long as possible.

Cameron advised him to watch the original movies, and skip the prequels. Always a movie buff, Elvis watched them all in the order they were released. He didn't see why Cameron had dismissed the prequels out of hand. They were amazing movies. The only mistake he could see was limiting the screen time of Jar Jar Binks in episodes II and III. Elvis thought Jar Jar was a hoot.

After watching all three of the movies in the original Star Wars trilogy, Elvis finally got a few hours of sleep. At ten o'clock the next morning, he was dressed and ready to make news.

The outfit Cameron had brought him to wear was made

of black leather. It was quite similar to the one he'd worn in 1968 for his special on NBC, his official comeback into the world of music.

Initially, he'd wanted to have new white sequined bell-bottom jumpsuits made for his return. Cameron had talked him out of it.

"We need to be forward thinking," Cameron had said. "Those jumpsuits are relics of the seventies. We don't want people thinking of you as a thing of the past. They need to see you once again as the future of music. And trust me when I say that nothing screams 'stuck in the past' like rhinestones and bellbottoms."

"But I can keep the sideburns, right?"

"Elvis without his sideburns would be like peanut butter and banana sandwiches without the peanut butter."

"They're bad enough on whole wheat bread and toasted instead of fried," Elvis said.

"Then you know exactly what I'm talking about."

"I certainly do."

Victoria had made him a vegan version of his favorite snack. *Bland* was the nicest word he could use to describe it. Without frying it in bacon fat, the sandwich just wasn't the same.

Now Elvis stood with her and Fatu in the wings of the stage of the small auditorium of the ground floor of CEO Music. After making sure Elvis was ready, Cameron made his way out to the podium.

"Everything is going to go great," Victoria whispered in Elvis's ear.

"I hope so," Elvis said. His leg shook with nervous energy.

She put a tender hand on his leg to steady it.

"Relax," she said. "They're going to love you."

"Thank you all for coming today," Cameron said from

the podium to the assembled two dozen or so reporters.

"As you know, whenever I call for a press conference, the news is going to be big. And today, I have for you the biggest news in a long time. It may not be bigger than Jesus, but it's definitely bigger than The Beatles."

"Yeah, yeah," a reporter yelled. "Whatever."

Cameron gave him a glare that shut him up, then continued.

"As some of you may know, my ex-wife, Victoria Hadley, is one of the world's most prominent geneticists. While we have each taken different roads to success in life, in the last few months, our paths converged, which is why you're all here today. Her work has paved the way for the future of human cloning."

A female reporter stood up. "What did you do, Ogilvie? Find some DNA from parts of Michael Jackson's original nose and make a clone?"

"Now, that's not a bad idea," he said. "But why would I clone the King of Pop when I could clone the King of Rock and Roll?

"Ladies and gentlemen, it is my pleasure to reintroduce to you the resurrected King of Rock and Roll—Elvis Presley!"

Cameron stood back and, with a sweeping gesture of his left hand, directed the reporters to the offstage area.

Elvis stepped out of the shadows and entered the world once again.

CHAPTER 34

"GOOD AFTERNOON, LADIES AND GENTLEMEN," Elvis said as Cameron handed him a wireless mic.

The reporters stared at him in silence. What was going on here? Was he already flopping? Finally, the female reporter spoke up, but she addressed Cameron, not Elvis.

"Cut the BS, Ogilvie. That may be an incredible-looking impersonator, but that's not Elvis."

"Yeah," another said. "He's been dead and buried for forty years now."

"And this guy's way too fit to be Elvis," a third blurted out.

They weren't excited to see him. They didn't even believe that he was Elvis Presley.

Cameron leaned into the microphones. "I'm not the one you should be addressing your questions to," he said. "Mr. Presley here is."

"Okay," the female reporter said. "Are you the real deal? Are you Elvis?"

"I know it's probably hard to believe, but yes, ma'am, I am," Elvis said.

"And what's your birthday?" another reporter asked.

"January eighth."

"Of what year?"

"That'd be 1935."

"Then that makes you eight-two. Sorry, but you don't

look much past forty."

"Actually, I'm forty-two."

"Wait a minute," a chubby blonde man with a goatee said. "Didn't Elvis die at forty-two?"

Cameron stepped back in. "Not this time. This time, Elvis is living right, eating healthy, and ready to start rocking again."

"And how can you prove that?" the reporter asked.

"I don't have to prove it," Cameron said. He took a step back and nodded to Elvis. "He will."

As planned, Fatu came on stage with a guitar and brought it over to Elvis. Elvis put the guitar strap over his shoulder. Fatu moved a mic stand over to him.

"Thank you," Elvis said, putting the wireless mic in the stand's holder.

Fatu moved away without saying a word. All eyes were glued on Elvis.

Elvis strummed his guitar and took a deep breath. He looked offstage and locked eyes with Victoria. She smiled and gave him a wink. All of the reporters had whipped out their smart phones to record the performance.

"Here goes nothing," Elvis said, and started into his first hit, "That's All Right." As it ended, he transitioned into "Mystery Train."

When Elvis broke into "Heartbreak Hotel," he had everyone's attention. Now that he had it, he broke loose with "Don't Be Cruel," which then blended into "Jailhouse Rock." His hips and legs moved at a speed and ferocity that had not been seen in decades.

At the end of his ten-minute musical demonstration, Elvis was drenched in sweat. But he was also energized. He loved playing, even for a small crowd like this. He could play for hours if Cameron would let him. But that wasn't the plan.

Cameron stepped in front of Elvis and told the reporters,

"I'm afraid that's all for now. But don't worry—there's a lot more of Elvis coming in the very near future."

The reporters shouted their questions after them, but Cameron was already ushering Elvis backstage. Fatu stayed behind to discourage any reporters who may have been tempted to follow him. None did.

Backstage Elvis, asked Victoria, "How'd I do?"

"You were incredible," she said.

"Yes, you were," Cameron said.

"So what happens now?" Elvis asked.

"Now," Cameron said, "we let all those self-important hacks do their job and see how America responds to the return of Elvis Presley."

CHAPTER 35

Michael Prescott checked his phone after finishing his two-hour workout in the dojo before heading to the shower. He noticed a missed call from his mom. He called her back rather than wait until after he'd showered.

She answered on the second ring.

"Hi, Mom."

"Mikey, have you been watching the news?" she asked.

Michael instantly thought some sort of a terrorist attack or mass shooting had happened while he was training.

"No, I've been working out. What's happened?"

"They cloned Elvis," she said.

Michael wasn't sure he'd heard her right.

"They did what?"

"Some big record producer. He's cloned Elvis."

"Mom, that can't be. It's gotta be a publicity stunt."

"I don't think it is."

She seemed certain. If anyone would know, it was his mom.

"Okay, what channel did you see it on?" he asked.

"It's on all of them."

Wow. This was big. Could it be real? If all of the cable news channels were broadcasting the story, then they were taking it seriously.

"Okay, let me check it out and call you back."

She said goodbye and he clicked the call off. Michael

opened the Twitter app and hit the search icon. Sure enough, the top trending story was *Elvis Presley Cloned.*

Michael clicked the link to a tweet from Kurt Sizemore. It took him to an article on Sizemore's *Bring Rock Back* blog declaring, "Elvis is Back!" He scanned the article about music producer Cameron Ogilvie announcing that he and his ex-wife had created a clone of Elvis.

Michael went back into the Twitter stream. He found a video of the alleged clone and hit play. It immediately showed a man who looked remarkably like Elvis signing a medley of the King's classic hits. On top of that, the man moved like Elvis.

Michael wasn't sure what to think. His initial reaction was to disbelieve this. It had to be a hoax. But this guy was good. Really good. If he was a tribute artist, he would definitely put Michael's job at risk.

But why would a huge music producer like Cameron Ogilvie do a publicity stunt like this? He didn't need exposure. He didn't need the money. He certainly wouldn't be spending his time, money, and reputation to promote a tribute artist and falsely claim the man was a clone of Elvis.

No, this wasn't a tribute performance Michael was viewing. He had spent his entire career channeling Elvis for the fans. This guy wasn't channeling. This guy was doing much more.

He wasn't just singing these classic songs. The songs poured out of him, and not merely out of his mouth, but his entire body. The moves were right. The performance wasn't being mimicked. This was all original.

Michael had only seen one other person perform like this.

Granted, it hadn't been live, but on the thousands of hours of concert footage he'd studied throughout his life. There was only one person he knew who could sing and move like this so naturally.

As much as he wanted to deny it, he had to wonder—was this indeed the return of Elvis Presley?

CHAPTER 36

THE MEDIA HADN'T IMMEDIATELY BOUGHT into the legitimacy of the clone after the press conference. Most of their headlines and stories were skeptical, some downright disdainful and ridiculing of Cameron Ogilvie.

That hadn't stopped them from putting the story at the top of every website and radio and TV news shows. They had it trending on all social media platforms by the time the sun set on the West Coast. They knew a good lead when they saw it. Plus, if it turned out to be a hoax, they could produce ten times as much coverage destroying Cameron. He'd never sign another artist to his label again.

Kurt Sizemore's *Bring Rock Back* blog had been the exception.

The clone's performance at CEO Music had mesmerized the music blogger. He wrote an in-depth article comparing this Elvis to concert footage from throughout the years. He also used photographic analysis to show this person was physically identical to the late Elvis Presley.

Kurt concluded the article by writing:

> "If this isn't Elvis Presley, then I don't know anything about rock and roll. And if, as all the know-nothing talking heads are speculating, this is a sham perpetrated by Cameron Ogilvie, then I should probably find another profession."

His peers and higher-profile competitors immediately sent Kurt links to jobs he could get when he needed to find other work. Public opinion was definitely against him. Genetic scientists and specialists from all over the world weighed in on the potential of Dr. Hadley creating a clone of Elvis Presley.

The general consensus from these scholars was that while Victoria Hadley's research had taken cloning far in recent years, they did not believe she could have made the leap to cloning a human being as quickly as this. They insisted this was nothing more than a publicity stunt orchestrated by her and her ex-husband.

The day after the press conference, Elvis Presley's estate denounced the clone as a fraud. The estate demanded an apology from Cameron. He flatly refused.

The estate followed up by threatening to sue Cameron for falsely claiming he'd cloned Elvis. Skylar Kauffman took to the cable news circuit, stating that if the estate continued with its statements, it would be sued for slandering not only Cameron Ogilvie and Victoria Hadley, but also the clone of Elvis Presley.

The escalating war of words and lawsuit threats continued until the end of the week. That was when Cameron sprang his trap in the guise of an olive branch. He agreed to allow the estate to send scientists to examine the clone. If the clone was indeed Elvis, the estate would have to admit as such. If that wasn't the case, Cameron would share that information with the public and settle any claims the estate might have against him.

He had the estate right where he wanted them. If they refused to examine the clone, it would be a de facto admission of his legitimacy. The examination would prove the same thing. But the estate didn't believe Elvis had been cloned. They accepted Cameron's invitation and assembled a team of lawyers to prepare aggressive settlement demands.

The very scientists who had stated unequivocally that this could not be a clone of Elvis Presley came to Bio-Design to examine the subject. Under Victoria's close observation, they poked and prodded Elvis for hours. In the end, they discovered that this indeed was a perfect clone of the original Elvis, right down to his fingerprints. They pulled his DNA and compared it to a genetic sample provided by the estate.

Within days, all of these self-proclaimed experts issued retractions and corrections to their original statements. The clone's DNA was a one hundred percent match to that provided for testing by Elvis's estate.

The clone was Elvis Presley!

They didn't know for certain how Victoria had done it or how the clone could have matured as fast as he did, but they no longer disputed this was indeed the real deal.

Elvis fans around the world were ecstatic. The King—*their King*—was back!

Despite the admission that the clone was without a doubt Elvis Presley, and the public's gleeful excitement and acceptance at his return, politicians and special interests in Washington once again demonstrated how out of touch they were with common Americans.

The Democrats bemoaned the fact that life could be created out of nothing. The Republicans lamented that man should not be playing God. Both sides demanded federal charges be filed immediately for ignoring FDA cloning regulations. Their demands paralyzed the Justice Department. Who could they arrest or charge, and for what crimes?

Should they go after Victoria Hadley for making the clone? Cameron Ogilvie for financing this experiment? Or Elvis Presley for being illegally cloned?

Finally, the always controversial and never conventional

President Donald Trump waded into the issue and resolved it with a tweet:

> *I'm completely pardoning Elvis & those who cloned him. Elvis was always a terrific American & is a big part of making America great again. #ElvisLives*

For one of the few times since he assumed office, President Trump's approval ratings went up. The American people loved Elvis and wanted him back. Forty years of pent-up demand was a hard thing to fight against. And Cameron knew it would make him richer than he'd ever been.

After the press conference, sales of Elvis's songs and records and even his movies went through the roof on both Amazon and iTunes. Both services temporarily went down under the flood of demand.

Cameron hated that he wasn't receiving any of that money. Those properties had come about under contract with the original Elvis, not his clone. But the songs released next would come from his clone. The money he'd make from those recordings would be phenomenal.

It would all start with a concert on what would have been Elvis's eighty-third birthday. And that concert had to be a major hit, or nothing else would work.

PART IV

VIVA LAS VEGAS

CHAPTER 37

Las Vegas, Nevada
January 8, 2018

ELVIS STARED DOWN AT THE Strip from the window of his suite atop the Oasis Hotel and Casino. Like everything else in the world, Vegas had changed greatly during his absence.

"What's it like to be back here?" Kurt Sizemore asked him.

"Well, it's brighter than I remember. And certainly bigger," Elvis said.

He returned from the window and sat down on a sofa across from the rock blogger. Cameron sat in a nearby chair, going over things on his iPad. He didn't seem to be paying attention, but Elvis had learned that Cameron caught everything.

That was why Kurt sat in the suite now. He'd treated Elvis with respect. Cameron had rewarded him for his articles by granting him an exclusive interview before the concert. And there weren't any grand rules. Any topic Kurt wanted to bring up was fair game.

"Do you mind if ask some personal questions?" Kurt said to Elvis.

"Fire away," Elvis said. "I ain't got nothing to hide."

"It's well known that you indulged in a variety of prescription drugs—"

"Yeah, I did. But that was a different time and I've

stopped taking them. I'm one hundred percent clean and intend to stay that way."

"That's good to hear. Now, your estate does not recognize you as Elvis Presley. You're barred from the Graceland property. Your ex-wife and your daughter refuse to see you or talk with you. And the estate has threatened legal action against you if you attempt to contact them or any family members or surviving members of your inner circle. What do you say to this?"

What Elvis wanted to say was how much it hurt him. How coming back to life meant nothing without the people who mattered most to him. But he and Cameron had discussed this. That wouldn't be the best answer for the public. Nor for his family. They needed to see that this indeed was Elvis. He needed to be above the controversy and be the kind, loving, magnanimous person they remembered him to be.

"Obviously, I wish that weren't the case," Elvis said, "but I understand where they're coming from."

"You do?"

"The me they knew, he died forty years ago. For me to spring up now like this without no warning, well, that's gotta take some getting used to. I know it did for me."

"But what if they never get used to the idea? What if they never want to have any interactions with you?"

That thought depressed Elvis more than anything. It left a hollow spot in his soul, an emptiness that he hadn't felt since his mother had died. However, he couldn't let that out. He had to be strong, just like the song he'd once recorded, "Only the Strong Survive."

"My whole life, people told me not to get my hopes up 'cause things wouldn't work out like I wanted. They told me not to quit driving for Crown Electric 'cause I'd never make any money as a singer. They told me that if I didn't stop moving around on stage, I'd never make it big. They told me that if I didn't find a way to get a deferment from the draft, I'd never have a career after I got out of the Army. They told me I'd never make it in Hollywood and to stick to singing. I maybe should've listened to them on that one, 'cause they told me I'd never get people to come see me sing again after making so many of those singing travelogues, but who else was seen live in concert before a billion people? So now they're telling me that no one will ever want to see me perform because I'm just a copy and that my family will never want nothing to do with me. Well, sir, if my life's any indication of how all those predictions are going to work out, then I'm probably on the right path. Heck, the fact that I'm sitting here with you right now ought to be proof enough of that."

CHAPTER 38

THE CONCERT THAT EVENING AT the T-Mobile Arena started as so many of his had. The band Cameron had put together played the opening of "Also sprach Zarathustra," the theme from *2001: A Space Odyssey*.

The capacity audience fell into a hush when Elvis strode out on stage. But rather than applaud, the audience held up their phones. What the heck were they doing? Fatu handed Elvis his guitar. He put the strap around his shoulder and approached the microphone.

The song changed and Elvis started singing "See See Rider," which morphed into "That's All Right." Rather than ending the song, Elvis continued the medley with Prince's "Let's Go Crazy" and Ricky Martin's "Livin' la Vida Loca."

Elvis and the band wrapped up the medley and he stared out at the crowd. They remained quiet. Had he just bombed? Could it be that the musical tastes of the people had changed so much that they no longer wanted Elvis?

All these doubts and fears vanished when the room erupted. The entire audience sprang to its feet, screaming and clapping with abandon. Elvis could see a few older women in the front row dabbing tears from their eyes. They loved him.

"Thank you. Thank you very much," Elvis said into the mic. The audience cheered louder. After nearly two minutes, they finally calmed down and Elvis spoke again.

"Good evening, ladies and gentlemen. My name is Justin Timberlake." The audience laughed. "I'm just kidding you. I'm actually Englebert Humperdinck." Again, laughter filled the auditorium. As he had so many times in the countless shows he'd done in the past, Elvis used humor to connect with his audience.

"What do you say we do some more songs?" he asked.

The audience cheered with approval. Elvis then sang "Hound Dog." After that, he did "Heartbreak Hotel," "Jailhouse Rock," and "All Shook Up."

After the collection of his early hits, stagehands wheeled a white piano out to center stage. Elvis sat down at the bench and played a random warm-up exercise on the keys. Fatu adjusted the microphone in its stand to bring it closer to Elvis's mouth.

"I'll tell you, I was a bit scared about coming out here tonight....yeah, at first you might say I was afraid...heck, maybe I was even a bit petrified."

Elvis played the piano and sang "I Will Survive," and as that song ended, he went into a piano-led rendition of "Sweet Child o' Mine." At the end of the two songs, he stood up and walked to the edge of the stage. Most people in the audience still held up their portable phones, pointed at him. This was so weird, but Elvis could tell they loved the show.

"Some of you might know I got my start back in 1954 with Sun Records, which was owned by Mr. Sam Phillips. Some say he's the man who invented rock and roll. I don't know about that. I think *discovered* might be a better word. And Mr. Phillips did discover some pretty incredible musicians. I knew them all, but while I was gone, a lot of them passed away themselves. Mr. Phillips too. So I'd like to do a little tribute to him and some of those great performers who used to record over at Sun Records there on Union Avenue in Memphis."

Fatu brought Elvis his guitar again. Once the strap was over his shoulder, Elvis launched into medley. First, he did "Blue Suede Shoes" by Carl Perkins, then sang "Ring of Fire" by Johnny Cash, and followed that with "A Cat Called Domino" by Roy Orbison. He finished with "California Boogie" by Howlin' Wolf.

The audience roared once again and rose to give Elvis another standing ovation.

"Thank you. Thank you very much, ladies and gentlemen."

Next on the set list was "Suspicious Minds." Elvis gave it everything he had, just like in the seventies. He followed that with a cover of the Santana/Rob Thomas collaboration "Smooth." After that, he performed "Burning Love."

"I've always been a huge fan of gospel music. And I heard this song that really touched me. It's by a group called MercyMe. It's called 'I Can Only Imagine,' and I'd like to play it for you now."

Elvis did "I Could Only Imagine." He followed it with "Tears in Heaven." As he sang, images of the family members, friends, and performers who had passed on came up on the screen.

"I was also a fan of country. Heck, when I was growing up in the South, that's all you were supposed to listen to if you were white. Well, I didn't quite follow that. I always liked the blues. I guess you could say I was a bit different, that I was standing outside the fire."

With that, Elvis performed a cover of the Garth Brooks song "Standing Outside the Fire." The audience loved it.

Elvis then closed out his show with "My Way."

As the song concluded, he left the stage. But unlike in times past, Elvis did not leave the building. He stood at the back of the stage listening to the thousands in the audience chant his name.

"El-vis...El-vis...El-vis."

Cameron had told him they'd expect an encore. They clearly did. After another thirty seconds, Elvis returned to the stage. The audience was even more excited than it had been before.

"I guess you want some more," he said into the mic.

The crowd roared a collective yes.

The first encore song was "Hey Ya!" by OutKast. Elvis got down and wild when it came time to shake it like a Polaroid picture.

"Thank you very much, ladies and gentlemen. You know, back in 1958, I was drafted into the Army. I did two years in the service. Guess that turned out all right, as we don't have no Soviet Union to worry about no more. And we ain't got no draft no more, either. But we still got a lot of bad folks who'd like to see America just go away. Fortunately, there's a lot of good men out there—and women, these days—doing their part to keep us safe and protect this great country that we all love. I'd like to do a song for them now."

Elvis sang his version of Toby Keith's "American Soldier." The song touched many people. Tears filled the audience. Elvis had hit all the emotional notes.

"Thank you. Thank you very much. You've been a wonderful audience. If we never meet again, may God bless you and a-dios."

With that, Elvis went into the closing song, bringing his performance to an end the way he always had for countless shows, by singing "Can't Help Falling in Love."

CHAPTER 39

ELVIS HAD BEEN EXTREMELY NERVOUS before his concert, but now he was reinvigorated. A powerful jolt of life had shot through him while on stage.

Elvis always enjoyed performing before a live audience. He'd gone on stage numerous times in his career when the stakes had been high, but perhaps never this high. Yet, as he had so many times before, he'd pulled it off.

And he'd pulled it off without the need for any pills.

Cameron had wanted to go out and celebrate, but they all knew they wouldn't be able to enjoy themselves. Out in public, Elvis knew people would swarm him, like they had done for more than twenty years. They decided to all call it a night and find a way to celebrate when they were back in Los Angeles.

Elvis returned to his suite alone, saying he felt like just watching some TV and getting a good night's sleep. Five minutes later, there was a knock at his door. He opened one of the double doors to find Victoria standing there, as they had arranged.

"I really owe you a lot," Elvis said as they sat down on the suite's large circular sofa.

"You don't owe me a thing," she said.

"Yes, I do. Without you helping me straighten up and getting me to live a healthy lifestyle, none of this would have been possible."

She smiled and moved nearer to him. "You're the one who had to make the decision to change."

"And you're the one who showed me it was possible. And you showed me how to make it happen. That means the world to me."

"Well, you're welcome."

Victoria moved in to kiss him, but Elvis pulled away. He got up and went into the master bedroom of the suite.

"Where are you going?" she asked.

"I've got something for you," he called back.

Elvis returned with a small gift-wrapped box. He offered it to her.

"You didn't need to do that," she said.

"Yeah, but that's what gifts are all about."

Victoria took the present from him. Gently, she unwrapped it, not tearing the paper at all. She opened the box to discover a gorgeous diamond tennis bracelet.

"Elvis...this is too much."

"No, I think it's just right," he said. He took it out of the box and put it around her wrist.

"It's beautiful."

"Just like the lady whose wrist it's now on."

She looked at him and smiled. "How did you get this?"

"On that Amazon website."

"I thought Cameron had cut you off."

"Oh, yeah, he did. But he also said I could keep the jewelry. I just didn't tell him that it weren't all for me."

"This is extremely kind and thoughtful of you. I'm not usually much of a jewelry person."

"I noticed that, but if you're going to be with me, you'd best get used to it."

Victoria kissed him. The kiss grew very passionate. Then the doorbell to the suite chimed.

"How's that for timing?" Elvis said with a grin.

"It's probably your dinner."

"I ain't too hungry. At least not for food." He looked at her lustily.

Victoria pushed herself away from him and headed for the doors. "Well, I actually had them put something special together for you tonight."

"Oh, you didn't need to do that," Elvis said.

"I didn't, but you can consider it a gift too."

Victoria opened the doors. A waiter wheeled in a cart with a silver-topped tray. He brought it over to Elvis. The waiter was all smiles and couldn't stop staring.

"You're really him," the waiter said. "You're really Elvis."

"That's what all them blood tests say," Elvis said.

"I can't believe I'm meeting you."

"You want an autograph?" Elvis asked.

"Would it be too much to take a selfie with you?"

"Take a what-ie?" Elvis asked.

Victoria joined them. "Give me your phone," she said to the waiter. "I'll take one of you two."

The waiter handed his phone to her and stood with Elvis. Elvis put his arm around the young man and Victoria snapped the picture.

"Thank you," the waiter said, taking his phone back. "If you need anything else, let me know."

"I will," Elvis said. "I don't have any cash on me, so why don't you add a tip to the room for two hundred dollars?"

"I will! Thank you so much."

The grinning waiter hurried out the doors, staring at the picture on his phone.

"So, what's my special meal?" Elvis asked Victoria when they were alone again.

"Take the lid off and find out."

Elvis did. Sitting on the plate was a grilled sandwich.

"Is that what I think it is?" he asked her. It couldn't be.

"One peanut butter and banana sandwich, fried specially for the King."

"In bacon fat, like my mama used to make?" he asked hopefully.

Victoria shook her head. "Peanut oil. I couldn't go that far. Hopefully, you enjoy it. After everything you've done, you deserved a treat."

"Thank you, Vicky Lynn. You're the best."

Elvis leaned over and kissed her, then picked up the sandwich and took a bite. It wasn't the best he'd ever had, but it sure beat the heck out of that vegan attempt Victoria had made that one time back in LA.

All things considered, this second chance at life was working out pretty good, Elvis thought. He smiled and took another bite of the sandwich.

CHAPTER 40

MICHAEL PRESCOTT WAS FAR FROM thrilled about the cloning of Elvis and the concert that had gone down in his adopted hometown.

The day after the clone's debut concert, the Oasis Casino placed *One Night with Elvis* on permanent hiatus. It infuriated Michael that after all the money he'd made the Oasis, they didn't even have the courtesy to deliver the news over lunch or even with a phone call. They notified him by email.

To add insult to this grievous injury, word leaked to the local press that the Oasis was attempting to lure the Blue Man Group to replace Michael's show. Michael had never felt this low in his life. He felt completely alone and worthless.

But he wasn't alone in this sentiment.

The clone's triumphant performance had wreaked havoc on all the Elvis tribute artists across America. With a clone of the real Elvis now on the scene, there wasn't a need for those who could merely channel Elvis in shows, birthday parties, or bar mitzvahs. Since Las Vegas had the largest number of tribute artists per capita, their community took the hardest hit. Venues across Sin City laid off their Elvis tribute artists and sought replacements for their acts.

Local 369 of the American Federation of Musicians did its best to find these suddenly out-of-work tribute artists new gigs. Those who could play instruments were directed toward house bands. Others received instructions to change their looks and impersonate other now-dead performers. This should have made finding new work easy for Michael. He was a talented musician and an incredible vocalist. He could have any gig he wanted.

But Michael Prescott didn't want any other gig. He'd been born to channel Elvis.

Ty and Eddie took Michael to dinner at his favorite steakhouse, the Nine at the Palms. On the few occasions when Michael ate red meat, it was a steak at the Nine. They hoped that a medium-rare bone-in rib eye would break him out of his funk.

"Come on," Ty said after they were seated in a booth. "It's not all bad. We got Elvis back. And it's really him!"

"Yeah," Eddie said. "And he's awesome."

Michael glared across the table at Eddie. "You went to that show?"

Eddie sank back in his seat. "I couldn't resist," he said. "It's Elvis."

"There's a lot of other work out there," Ty said. "With Elvis back, a lot of places are looking to put plenty of other tribute artists on stage. I've got an audition to play Prince on Thursday."

This baffled Michael. "Ty, you're white."

"I know, it's a bit of a long shot, but they like the way I play the guitar, and Prince wore a ton of makeup. I think I can pull it off."

"I heard the Station's looking to put a country legends show together," Eddie said. "You could nail Johnny Cash."

"Not interested," Michael said.

"Yeah. I see you more as a Merle Haggard," said Ty.

"If you grew a beard, you could pull of Waylon Jennings," said Eddie.

Ty nodded his agreement. "I can totally see that."

"I'm not interested," Michael said, and slid out of the

booth.

"What are you going?" Eddie asked.

"Home," Michael said.

"We ain't even ordered yet," Ty said.

"Not hungry," Michael said.

"Mikey, come on," Eddie said as he got out of the booth too. "The times are changing. If you're going to make it, you've got to change with them."

"You two can change all you want," Michael said. "I'm not. I was born to be Elvis."

Michael turned his back on Ty and Eddie, and walked out of the restaurant.

"Well, that went great," Ty said as Eddie sat back down. "What are we going to do now?"

"Give him time," Eddie said. "Sooner or later, he's gonna face the reality that his days of being Elvis are over."

CHAPTER 41

"CLONE OF ELVIS IS THE Real Rockin' Deal" proclaimed *Rolling Stone* the day after the concert. All the other outlets ran similar stories, finally admitting what they'd been denying for months.

Kurt Sizemore, however, had his exclusive interview with the resurrected King of Rock and Roll. This gave his site its biggest day since he'd gone live.

Over a thousand videos from those attending the concert were uploaded to YouTube. By noon the next day, over ten million people had viewed the different videos.

And once the show had ended, Cameron released the *Elvis Reborn* album exclusively on CEO Music's website. He wasn't about to share any of the profits with Jeff Bezos or Tim Cook. The album contained fifteen new Elvis songs. They weren't newly written songs, but covers of hit songs that had been released by various artists during the forty-year absence of Elvis. Some he'd sung live that evening. Others were held back for this album.

On the album were:

The House That Built Me

I Can Only Imagine

Sweet Child o' Mine

Tears in Heaven

Do You Really Want to Hurt Me?

One
Smooth
Black or White
Standing Outside the Fire
Livin' la Vida Loca
Hey Ya!
I Will Survive
If I Could Turn Back Time
Let's Go Crazy
Them Eyes

The new Elvis music knocked everyone else off the charts. These new songs became the highest grossing of his career. For the first time ever, the top ten songs on the charts were all by the same artist. The radio stations—top forty, pop, classic rock, and country—played the new Elvis songs more than once each hour.

Cameron's instincts had been proven right. People could not get enough of Elvis.

Artists who had originally stood with the estate or remained quiet on the topic of the clone were won over. They couldn't deny he was the King. When asked about the "Tears in Heaven" cover, Eric Clapton proclaimed Elvis's rendition superior to his own.

Those performers who had known Elvis or grown up under his influence began reaching out to Cameron's office. They all wanted to play with the clone. Bruce Springsteen asked if he could tour with Elvis. One of his dreams had always been to open for the King. He'd even write an album of original songs for Elvis as part of the deal.

Cameron politely told the Boss no. Elvis Presley didn't need an opening act. Elvis was his own opening, main, and encore act. Bringing Elvis back and putting him on tour had been Cameron's idea and his alone. No one was going to push their way in on it.

These were, without a doubt, the greatest days of Cameron Ogilvie's already incredible life. He wasn't about to share it with anyone else.

And that was exactly when things took a turn that threatened it all.

CHAPTER 42

MONDAY MORNING, WHEN THEY WERE all back in Los Angeles. Cameron had Fatu bring Elvis and Victoria to CEO Music's Century City office.

"Elvis, you're going to love what I've got planned," Cameron said. "This is going to be the tour of both of your lifetimes."

"You finally gonna get me to play in Europe?" Elvis asked as he took a seat across from Cameron's desk.

"You bet your gyrating pelvis I am," Cameron said. "And plenty of other places. Show him, fathead."

Fatu unfurled a large concert poster. It showed Elvis superimposed over the globe with locations and dates for concerts scheduled around the planet.

"Friday, we're going to announce a fifty-city worldwide tour," Cameron said.

"Fifty-city?" Elvis asked.

"That's right. Five shows in each city. I want everyone to get a chance to see you live. And also so the diehard fanatics can see you all five times in a row when you come to their town. It'll be incredible."

"That's two hundred and fifty shows in a year." Victoria said.

"It'll be the biggest concert tour ever," Cameron said. He pivoted his attention back to Elvis. "We'll kick things off in New York, back in Madison Square Garden, just like you did in the old days. *Saturday Night Live* wants you to host. It'll really be a boost to their ratings, and they'll pay handsomely for it. We'll also record more songs while we're back there. I'm thinking we'll title the next album *Return of the King*. We'll release it toward the end of the tour."

Elvis tried to speak, but Cameron kept talking.

"At the same time, we'll be filming and recording your concerts. When the tour's done, we'll edit the best parts into a movie and a concert album, just like you and Colonel Parker used to do."

"Yeah," Elvis said. "That's how the Colonel liked to do it. But I'm not so sure about all this."

"Elvis," Cameron said, "things move a lot faster now than they did in the '50s or even the '70s. We have to strike hard and fast now, or people will forget all about you."

"I understand that, Mr. Ogilvie, but one of the things I said when I signed with you is I wanted to do things different this time."

"I've let you pick your own music, and have I said one word about doing any movies other than the concert films?"

"No, sir, but what I'm talking about is the touring schedule. It's too much."

Cameron couldn't believe his ears. Was his clone really talking to him this way? He kept his cool and decided to explain things as clearly as possible.

"There's an incredible pent-up demand to see you live." Cameron pointed at the dates on the poster Fatu still held up. "This might actually be doing too little."

"I understand what you're saying," Elvis said. "But being on the tour so long is a big part of what wore me down before."

"Yes, but now you're sober and in much better shape than you've been in years."

Victoria spoke up. "He is. And if you want him to stay

that way, you might want to dial this back a bit, Cam."

Cameron gave Elvis and Victoria a stern look. They were not going to dictate terms to him. "The venues are already booked. The dates are set."

"Then the dates are going to need to be changed," Elvis said.

Cameron stared at Elvis. This dimwitted clone wasn't getting it. "Somehow I've given you the false impression that this schedule is up for negotiation. Let me be clear, it's not."

Elvis shook his head. "Then I'm sorry, Mr. Ogilvie. I'm not going on that tour without some big changes to the schedule."

Cameron stood up and bared his teeth like a snarling dog.

"Oh really?" Cameron asked.

"I'm afraid so," Elvis said.

Cameron's eyes narrowed and bored directly into Elvis's.

"Listen up, you pampered country bumpkin. You wouldn't be here if it wasn't for me. You will tour when and where I say you do."

"Cameron—" Victoria said.

"Stay out of it," Cameron said, keeping his eyes locked on the clone. "This is between me and him."

For a long moment, he and Elvis stared at each other without saying a word. Victoria shifted uncomfortably in her chair. Finally, Elvis stood.

"Then why don't you just forget about the whole dang tour," Elvis said.

"That's not going to happen," Cameron said.

"All right, then you're going to make some changes."

"The schedule stays as it is. And I'll remind you that we have a contract."

"Then I guess you can sue me," Elvis said, and turned for the door.

"For what?" Cameron asked. "You don't have any money. Everything you've made belongs solely to me."

This got Elvis's attention. He faced Cameron. Cameron smiled. He had the clone over a barrel, and it was time to let him know.

"You never were very bright," Cameron said. "Especially when it came to business and contracts. Our agreement specifically states all profits from this venture belong to me until you've completed the terms as I see fit. You'll forfeit it all if you dare to leave."

Victoria got to her feet. "What kind of a contract is that?" she asked.

"The kind he happily signed," Cameron said.

"That doesn't make him your slave," she said.

"Slave is such a harsh, out-of-date word," Cameron said. "The better word might be *experiment*. That's what you are, after all, Elvis. You're nothing more than a science experiment conducted by my ex and financed by my fortune. But since Dr. Frankenstein has started sleeping with her monster, she seems to have forgotten that."

Elvis pointed at Cameron and snarled. "You watch how you talk about her."

"Or what?" Cameron asked. "You'll karate chop me?"

Victoria took Elvis by his outstretched hand and lowered it. "Don't," she said. "He's not worth it."

Elvis took a breath and nodded. "You're right. He's not."

Elvis interlaced his fingers with Victoria's, then said, "Let's get out of here."

"I don't think so," Cameron said. "Fatu."

Fatu stepped in front of the door and blocked their exit.

"She can leave, and probably should," Cameron said to Elvis. "But you're not going anywhere. Except on this tour."

Elvis turned back to Cameron. "Man, you're one big sicko."

"The geniuses who've changed the world have often been ridiculed by their small-minded critics," Cameron said.

Victoria squeezed Elvis's hand. "Don't worry," she said. "I'm not going to let him do this to you."

"If that's the route you're going to take, then I'll consider it contract interference. In which case, I'm not going to be able to provide the funding you need for Phase Two of your research."

"I don't care about your money," she said. "I care about him."

"And which *him* is that now?" Cameron asked.

Fire filled Victoria's eyes. "Don't you even dare go there."

"Don't worry," Cameron said without emotion. "I won't. Our business is now concluded. Now you'll get out and leave me and my clone to ours."

PART V

IT'S NOW OR NEVER

CHAPTER 43

VICTORIA HADN'T LIED TO ELVIS. She wasn't going to let Cameron get away with what he was attempting. At least not without giving him a major fight.

She reached out to a fellow Stanford alumnus, Michelle "Mitchi" Magaña. Mitchi had gone on to law school and built a solid reputation for herself in the areas of immigration and human rights. While Victoria and Mitchi hadn't touched base in years, she did not hesitate to take Elvis on as a client. This could earn her a place in the history books and possibly a seat on the federal bench. The outcome of his case would have severe implications on human rights and cloning in the years to come.

Mitchi got a hold of Elvis. Once he agreed to have her as his counsel, she immediately filed a temporary restraining order in federal court against Cameron Stone and CEO Music. The TRO would derail the trip to New York and the beginning of the tour.

Cameron, as expected, was furious. He ordered Skylar Kauffman to resolve this as quickly as possible.

Skylar appeared two days later in Los Angeles federal court before Judge Timothy Rentz to quash the TRO.

"Your Honor, this TRO is completely out of bounds," Skylar began.

"How so, counselor?" Judge Rentz asked from his perch on the bench.

"First, the subject in question is a clone. A clone does not have the same rights as a naturally born human being."

"Your Honor, that's ridiculous," Mitchi said.

"The only thing ridiculous is this hearing," Skylar said. "A clone does not have any standing before this court or any other."

Before Mitchi could respond, Judge Rentz nodded. "I do believe that's what we're here to decide."

Judge Rentz set a hearing on the matter at the end of the week. The court would hear arguments as to whether the clone of Elvis Presley did have the same rights and protections that the original Elvis Presley had enjoyed when he lived.

If the cloning of Elvis Presley was a major media story, then the court hearing received even greater attention.

The morning of the hearing, the courtroom was filled with reporters and fans who had to get a look at Elvis as he sat at the petitioners' table with Mitchi. Victoria held a seat in the gallery behind Mitchi and Elvis. Cameron sat at the adjacent table with Skylar Kauffman, who would either earn his money or be proven right when he'd warned Cameron against the contract he'd had the clone sign.

The first witness Mitchi called was, of course, Elvis. After he was sworn in, she began her questioning.

"Mr. Presley, when were you born?"

"January 8, 1935," Elvis said.

"Objection," Skylar said. "If the witness was born in 1935, he'd be over eighty years old. This individual is obviously not eighty."

"Sustained," the judge said. "Please restate your question."

"When do you believe you were born?" Mitchi asked.

"January 8, 1935. But I was reborn on July 17, 2017, if that makes Mr. Kauffman happy."

"And where were you born?"

"Objection," Skylar said. "This is irrelevant. Both parties stipulate that this is a clone, but clones are not born as natural human beings are."

Judge Rentz looked to Mitchi, who was already answering. "Opposing counsel is trying to derail my questions with issues of semantics."

"I'll allow the question," the judge said. "Let's keep things moving." He looked at Elvis and nodded.

"The first time, I was born in Tupelo, Mississippi," Elvis said. "The second, well, not too far from here in Dr. Hadley's lab over at Bio-Design."

Elvis gave Victoria a wink when he said it. She smiled and looked down.

"Are you a United States citizen?" Mitchi asked.

"Proudly so," Elvis said.

"And as a citizen of the United States, were you drafted into the United States Army?"

"Yes, ma'am. I was inducted in March of 1958."

"Your Honor—" Skylar said.

"Mr. Kauffman," Judge Rentz said. "We all know this is an unprecedented matter. I'm giving Ms. Magaña a certain amount of latitude. I'll do the same for you."

Mitchi smiled at that small admonishment to her opposition.

"And when did your service conclude?" she asked Elvis.

"In 1960. But I was in active reserve until 1964."

"And were you honorably discharged?"

"Yes, ma'am."

Mitchi took a paper from her files and approached the bench. "Your Honor, I'd like to enter into the record the DD-214 for Elvis Presley, demonstrating the testimony of my client is accurate."

"I object to that admission," Kauffman said. "This a

record pertaining to the original Elvis Presley, not this clone."

"I stipulate that the man sitting here today is a clone of Elvis Presley," Mitchi said. "However, Elvis Presley was also an American citizen, as proven by the fact that the United States government drafted him into the military. If we are debating the merits of this individual's citizenship, then the court must also look at the citizenship of the person from whom this clone was produced."

Skylar immediately countered her contention: "How the original Elvis Presley was or wasn't viewed by the federal government sixty years ago is not relevant to the issue before us today."

"Actually, counselor," Judge Rentz said, "since all parties have stipulated that this is indeed a clone of the late Elvis Presley, I do believe such information is germane to these proceedings."

Mitchi turned to smile at Skylar, and he sat down. Cameron leaned over and whispered into his attorney's ear.

"Letting that draft issue get by you had better not bite me in the ass."

"They were always going to get it through," Skylar said. "But that's good. It just opened an important door for us."

CHAPTER 44

SKYLAR KAUFFMAN DIDN'T HAVE MANY questions for Elvis. Little that the clone could say would serve his client's case. His star witness, however, would be the one they'd least expect: Victoria Hadley herself.

The bailiff swore in Victoria and she climbed into the witness stand beside the judge's bench.

"Dr. Hadley," Skylar began. "Did you produce the clone of Elvis Presley we see sitting here today?"

"I did," she said.

"And how is this thing we see sitting here—"

"Objection," Mitchi said from her seat. "It is improper for counsel to refer to Mr. Presley as a thing rather than a person."

"Withdrawn," Skylar said before the judge could speak. "How is this person we see sitting here any different from Elvis Presley?"

"He's in much better shape, he's not a hypochondriac, and he's physically lived several months longer than the other Elvis did."

"The other Elvis?"

"Yes. The original Elvis."

"Right. But in what ways is this duplicate of the original different than what you've so proudly listed for us?"

"He's not. He's a perfect copy. For all intents and purposes, he is Elvis Presley."

Skylar walked closer to the witness box. "Would you venture to say that he's human?"

"I absolutely would," Victoria said.

"No different than you or I?"

"Not at all."

Skylar plucked a hair out of his head and held it before Victoria's face.

"If I were to give you this strand of my hair, Dr. Hadley, could you theoretically produce an exact copy of the me that is standing here questioning you at this moment?"

"Your question's not theoretical. I could create an exact clone of you," Victoria said, then added, "Just as I did with Elvis."

"And that clone would be identical to me in every way?"

"One hundred percent."

Skylar grinned. He had her and she didn't even know it.

"Would that include the duplication of my memories?" he asked.

"Up until the point when you plucked that follicle, yes."

"And do you think my wife would know it wasn't me if my clone came home and took her out to dinner at Mastro's?"

"Unless she was told so, no."

"All right, then let us say my hypothetical clone takes my wife to dinner, they have a wonderful time, return home, and make love."

"Objection, your Honor," Mitchi said. "This line of question is way out of line."

"Your Honor," Skylar said, "I had the understanding that you'd give us each a fair amount of leeway."

"And I will," Judge Rentz said. "But you're going to need to get to your point, counselor."

"I certainly shall, your Honor," Skylar said. He turned his full attention back to Victoria. "So my clone and my wife come home from a nice night out and they make love. Could she become pregnant in the encounter?"

He saw the flicker of fear in her eyes. She'd fallen directly into his trap.

"I've never examined your wife and wouldn't know—"

Skylar cut her off. He was not going to let her evade his question. "My wife has had four children with me and we're discussing having another. Could a clone of me father that child with her?"

Victoria looked down. She didn't answer.

"Dr. Hadley?" he asked.

"No," she said in a lower voice, without looking up.

"And why not?"

Victoria finally looked up. The anguish was evident on her face. "Human clones are unable to naturally reproduce."

"And why is that?"

"I don't know. It might have something to do with the growth enhancers, or perhaps it's the complexity of the genome for primates and humans that inhibits the replication of reproductive abilities."

Skylar pointed at Elvis. "Then are you saying that this clone of Elvis cannot father a child?"

Victoria looked Elvis in the eye, then looked away before answering, "No."

"But didn't you say in your testimony that this clone is an exact copy of Elvis Presley?"

"He is."

Skylar went to his table. Cameron looked up at him with a victorious grin. Skylar picked up two documents from his papers.

"Your Honor, I'd like to enter into the record two documents," Skylar said. "The first is a marriage certificate issued by Clark County, Nevada for Elvis Aron Presley and Priscilla Beaulieu from 1967. The second is a birth certificate for a Lisa Marie Presley, born on February 1, 1968 to Elvis and Priscilla Presley in Memphis, Tennessee."

"Objection, your Honor," Mitchi said as she stood. "These documents have absolutely nothing to do with the matter before the court."

"Your Honor, the court found Mr. Presley's military service record germane to these proceedings," Skylar said. "We believe these documents are of similar interest to the court."

Rentz mulled it over then nodded. "I'll allow their admission."

Skylar brought the documents over to the witness box and placed them before Victoria.

"According to these documents, Dr. Hadley, would you agree that Elvis Presley, the real Elvis Presley, produced offspring with his ex-wife, Priscilla, a daughter by the name of Lisa Marie?"

She didn't look at them before answering. "Everyone knows that's true."

"Yes, they do. And by your own admission, we now see that the clone of Elvis is not an exact duplicate of the real Elvis."

"He's as real as Elvis ever was," she said.

"Yet he can't reproduce. Don't you believe that's a rather significant difference, doctor?"

"It's the only difference."

"Is it? Who is this clone's mother?"

His question threw her off, and it took her a moment to answer. "I believe her name was Gladys."

"It was," Skylar said. "And did Gladys Presley give birth to this clone sitting here today?"

"Technically, no."

"Yet she did give birth to the man we all know as Elvis Presley?"

"And his twin brother Jesse."

"But she didn't give birth to this clone, this fake, this imposter, sitting before us today, now did she?"

"Objection, your Honor," Mitchi said. "Argumentative."

But Skylar had gotten under Victoria's skin, as he'd intended, and she still responded.

"He's as much a human being as you or my ex-husband," she said with defiance. "Possibly more so."

"Thank you for your opinion, doctor," Skylar said. "But I believe that's what we're here for the court to decide."

CHAPTER 45

ELVIS AND VICTORIA WAITED FOR Judge Rentz to issue his tentative ruling in a side room of the federal courthouse. Mitchi had arranged the private room for Elvis to spare him from the mob of media and fanatics that swarmed him every time he stepped outside the courtroom. She had lunch brought in for them, healthy and vegan, per Victoria's instructions.

While Mitchi stepped out to return calls to her office, Elvis sat with Victoria to share the afternoon meal. Uncharacteristically, he didn't touch his food. He wasn't hungry.

"What is it?" she asked.

Elvis took a few seconds before he answered her with a question of his own. "So clones can't have babies, huh?"

"No, they can," Victoria said. "It's only primate and human clones that can't. And don't ask me why, because I don't know. Like I said on the stand, it could be a side effect of the growth enhancers, or the genomes of both species are too complex for us to properly replicate yet."

Elvis nodded as he processed this information. "How come you didn't bother to tell me?"

"I didn't think it would matter."

"It does matter," he said, and stood up. He faced the wall. He didn't want to look at her. "It kind of makes me feel like I ain't completely a man or something."

Victoria got to her feet and went around the table to stand beside him. "You're more of a man than most I've known in my life."

He still couldn't face her. "But I still can't have any babies."

"You want babies?"

"Well, after Lisa Marie and the rest of my family disowned me, it got me thinking that it'd be nice to have a family. Maybe get that part of my life right this time too. Especially if I had the right woman with me."

Elvis turned and looked her deeply in the eyes. She was so incredibly beautiful. And it wasn't merely her appearance. Everything about her he found beautiful. He was falling in love with her. He wanted Vicky Lynn by his side. Now and forever.

But Victoria turned away from him.

"I'm flattered, but I wouldn't be able to even if you could."

Her response threw Elvis. "But you're still young enough," he said.

"Physically I can, at least for a while longer, but..." Victoria shook her head.

Elvis put his hands on her shoulders, massaging them gently with his thumbs. "What is it, Vicky Lynn? Did I say something wrong?"

She shook her head. He took his hands off her and took a couple steps back.

"Then it's me, huh?"

Victoria turned to face him. "No," she said. "It's me."

Elvis remained bewildered. "Then you're saying with all that's been going on between us—"

"No. I've loved every minute with you. But even if we did get married and you could father a child, you wouldn't want to with me."

"Oh, I think I would."

"Do you remember my son I told you about?" she said, sadness creeping into her voice.

Elvis nodded. Of course he did.

"His name was Bryce," she said. "He was born with a rare disease called Hunter syndrome. Cameron and I didn't know that until he was two, but even if we had, it wouldn't have mattered."

Victoria looked down at the tile before saying, "He died a week before his fourth birthday."

Elvis saw tears form in her eyes, then fall onto her cheeks. He put his arms around her and pulled her close to him.

"I'm really sorry about that, Vicky Lynn."

"Don't be," she said, wiping the tears from her face. "There isn't anything anyone could have done. Including me, and I'm a doctor. Cameron completely blamed me for it."

"You know I'd punch in him in his fat mouth if I could," he said.

"We both would, but he wasn't entirely wrong," Victoria said. "Hunter's is a genetic disease and therefore hereditary. It's not on his side at all, but it turns out that it's on mine."

Elvis wasn't sure what he should say, or if he should say anything.

Victoria looked up at him with tear-filled eyes. "At least your mother had you after she lost Jesse. I couldn't even risk having another kid knowing that I'd likely passed it on to my little boy."

"You know, you shouldn't be beating yourself up like this," Elvis said.

"It helps keep me focused."

"On what?"

"On bringing him back," Victoria said.

She stepped out of Elvis's embrace and went over to the table. She opened her purse and dug inside for something.

"There's still work to be done on it, but I don't think it'll be too long before I can crack the code on defective chromosomes that cause Hunter's. Then I'll be able to create a genetic cure."

Victoria removed a clear plastic vial from her purse. She held it up for Elvis to see. It contained several long strands of light brown hair.

"And when I do that, I'm going to bring my Bryce back."

Elvis understood it all right now. She hadn't agreed to clone him simply because of the money Cameron had promised or to advance genetic science. Her reasons were deeply personal.

"That's why you got involved with Cameron in all this."

"I had to figure out how to clone a human first. And without his funding, it would have taken another decade or longer. That's why I made the deal with the damn devil incarnate himself."

"Well, I'm glad you did," Elvis said. "I wouldn't be here if you hadn't. And if that helps you bring back your little boy in good health, then that may be the most important thing I've ever done with my life. This one or the one I had before."

CHAPTER 46

"THIS CASE IS AN INTERESTING one, and even that is an obvious understatement," Judge Rentz said to the people packed into his courtroom.

Elvis looked behind him to Victoria. Several reporters snapped pictures when he did. Victoria nibbled on her bottom lip and held up her crossed fingers. Mitchi had put forward a strong case, but Skylar was a skilled attorney. Anything could happen now.

"As our science and our technologies advance," Rentz said, "I'm certain this is the first of many such cases our courts will be asked to rule on. And in those, like this one, our abilities will outpace legislation. Whatever I rule here will be precedent setting. I'm extremely aware of that, and I've deliberated over this most seriously."

Rentz took a breath then continued.

"The real question before the court is: what is human life? Some in our society believe life begins at conception. Others believe it begins at birth. But where does it begin for a clone that is neither conceived nor born, at least not in the manner we traditionally comprehend it?"

He let his words hang over the courtroom before speaking again.

"As we delve into this question, we must examine the hard facts of this matter. While this clone is undoubtedly an exact genetic replica of the late Elvis Presley, we can all see that parents did not conceive him. Nor was he born. Nor can he produce offspring.

"While there are many people in our society who cannot conceive for multiple reasons, there has never been a person that was not conceived nor born. Even the incarnation of Christ entered the world through the womb of a woman.

"This indeed is a legal conundrum the likes of which this court has never before encountered. It creates a serious constitutional question, especially since the law is silent on this matter. Perhaps we see exactly some of those reasons here before us today.

"As I have never been a proponent of legislating from the bench, I do not believe there is ample reason for me to step into the role of the people's representatives in this matter."

Judge Rentz sat up straight in his chair. He looked at Elvis. The clone stared back at him. Rentz averted his eyes and held them on the table where Cameron sat with Skylar.

"The court finds that while the defendant is indeed a genetic clone of the late Elvis Presley, he is not, in fact, Elvis Presley. Nor is he human by any definition that has ever existed in either natural or constitutional law. Therefore, I find for Mr. Ogilvie and CEO Music Incorporated."

Victoria could not believe this. Her mouth dropped open, but no words or sounds came out of her. They'd lost. Elvis legally belonged to Cameron, and he could do with the clone as he pleased.

In front of her, Cameron slapped his hand across Skylar's back. Mitchi pounded her fist against the table. Everyone in the gallery began to speak in loud voices. Rentz silenced them with two solid hits of his gavel, then continued his remarks.

"Until such time as Congress and the president change the law, the clone of Elvis cannot be defined under the law as a human being. He therefore does not enjoy the constitutional protections and civil liberties enjoyed by natural-born humans. This court is adjourned."

Rentz hit the gavel one more time. Everyone got to their feet. As the judge descended from the bench and went to his chambers, the once-placid courtroom became a madhouse of frenzied activity and rising voices.

Elvis remained seated at the table, stunned by the ruling. He closed his eyes tight. Photographers in the gallery snapped as many pictures as they could of his anguished expression.

"I told you that contract would hold up," Skylar told Cameron.

"As good as your word, Sky," Cameron said. "As good as your two-thousand-dollar-per-hour word!"

The smiling Cameron looked at Elvis, then walked over and stood in front of him. Every journalist snapped multiple pictures of the encounter.

"Well, my dimwitted and obstinate clone," Cameron said. "We should get back home and get you packed for your first world tour."

She couldn't take it anymore. Victoria jumped up and pushed through the small wooden gate. She went over to the table where Elvis still sat with Mitchi.

"We'll appeal this," she said to Elvis, then turned to Mitchi. "We can appeal it, right?"

"I'll have something filed with the Ninth Circuit tonight," Mitchi said.

"Speaking of filing things with the courts," Cameron said to Victoria, "I believe Fatu has something for you."

Fatu stepped out of the crowd and pulled a folded document from the inside pocket of his suit coat. He handed it to Victoria.

"What the hell is that?" Victoria asked the bodyguard.

Fatu said nothing. Skylar, however, answered her

question.

"That is a restraining order prohibiting you from being within two hundred feet of both Cameron Edmund Ogilvie and his clone of Elvis Presley. Any contact you have or attempt to have with them will be a violation of this order."

Victoria stared at the paper in her hand. "Cameron, please," she said.

Cameron brushed her away with a flip of his fingers.

"You really should get going, Vic, or we'll have to have one of these fine deputies take you into custody."

Victoria knew he wasn't bluffing. In stunned silence, she backed away from Elvis and returned to the gallery. A reporter was immediately upon her.

"Dr. Hadley, how do you feel about this ruling?" the reporter asked. She ignored him and pushed her way back into the gallery and toward the doors. Before exiting, she looked back in at Elvis. He sat back down in his chair and hung his head low.

She'd never seen Elvis look this sad.

CHAPTER 47

Judge Rentz's ruling devastated Michael Prescott, possibly as much as it did Elvis. At his house, he sat between Eddie and Ty on the living room sofa. The flat screen on the wall showed CNN's legal analysts discussing the ruling the trio had watched live.

A glimmer of hope had returned to Michael when he'd learned the clone wanted out of his deal with Cameron Ogilvie. Maybe that damned abomination would stop singing and vanish. That would revive the demand for tribute artists. Michael would get his gig and his life back.

But Judge Rentz incinerated all such hopes.

Eddie picked the remote up from the coffee table and shut off the TV. "Well, that's that," he said, and stood up.

"Yeah. I guess it really is time to move on," Ty said as he also got to his feet.

Michael stayed planted on the couch. Ty and Eddie both stared down at him.

"No," Michael finally said. "I'm not giving in."

"Oh, come on," Eddie said. "Get a damn clue. Elvis isn't going anywhere but on a massive tour and up the charts."

Michael jumped up and pointed his finger at Eddie's face. "Don't you call him Elvis! That's not the real Elvis. He's a fake!"

Ty put his hand on Michael's shoulder and asked, "And what were we?"

"We are his loyalists," Michael said. "We are his army. We kept his flame alive for his fans."

"Yeah, *his* fans," Ty said. "Not ours. And now they don't need us, because they've got him again."

"Come on, Mike," Eddie said. "It's time to hang up the bellbottoms, wash the dye out of our hair, and shave our sideburns. It's time for us all to leave the building."

"I can't believe you two," Michael said. "How can you give up so easily? It's not over yet."

Eddie grabbed Michael by the shoulders and shook him hard. "It was over for us the moment they hatched him out of his test tube, Mike!"

"I don't believe that."

Eddie looked over to Ty. "Did you bring them?"

Ty lifted his backpack. "Got 'em right here."

Ty reached into the bag and removed a pair of electric clippers.

"What are you doing with those?" Michael asked. Fear and anxiety rose within him.

"Shaving our sideburns," Eddie said.

"You're not touching my chops," Michael said.

"You think I want to do this?" Ty asked. "I love Elvis as much as you do, but we've got to move on."

"It'll be easier if we all shave them together," Eddie said.

Michael took a step away from Ty. "You stay the hell away from me."

With a fast move, Eddie grabbed Michael and pinned his arms behind him.

"Let me go!" Michael yelled.

"Right after Ty's done."

Ty turned the clippers on. They buzzed loudly as he brought them near Michael's head.

Michael couldn't let them do this. He had to get away. If he lost his sideburns, he'd be set back years as a tribute artist.

"I'll do it quick," Ty told Michael. "Just like ripping off a Band-Aid."

Michael responded by letting out a loud warrior scream. He jumped up, using Eddie's grasp as leverage, and kicked the clippers out of Ty's hand. Michael then threw himself forward and flipped Eddie over his back.

Eddie landed hard on his right side. He sat up, rubbing his ribs.

Michael went into a fighting stance. Ty and Eddie looked over at their friend.

"What the hell's the matter with you?" Eddie asked.

"That's the difference between me and you," Michael said. "You love Elvis. That's why you can act like him. But it's more than that for me. I *am* Elvis."

"No, you're not!" Eddie said.

Michael curled his lip and motioned with his fingers for Eddie to get up. This time when Michael spoke, he did so in the voice he used when channeling Elvis. "Then get up and come get some more, son."

Eddie stayed on the carpet. Michael backed away from Ty and Eddie, not taking his eyes off them as he grabbed his car keys from the hook by the front door.

"Where do you think you're going now, Looney Toons?" Eddie said.

"To make things right again," Michael said.

"How you going to do that?" Ty asked.

"Don't you worry about that," Michael said. "But both you boys will be thanking me when it's done."

Michael opened the door and rushed outside.

CHAPTER 48

THAT EVENING AT CAMERON'S MANSION, preparations were underway for the trip to New York City. Whether he wanted to do it or not, Elvis would soon be hosting *Saturday Night Live* and launching his first worldwide tour. Whatever Cameron ordered, Elvis now had no other choice but to obey the man.

Elvis studied himself in the full-length mirror in the bedroom. He looked fantastic. Better than he had since he got out of the Army. But it didn't matter. His face showed the immense sadness now overwhelming his heart.

He couldn't deny that his life had gone horribly wrong all over again. He'd been doing everything different this time around. Yet here he was, once again trapped by his own fame and tied to a man even more self-serving and manipulative than Colonel Parker.

How could that have happened?

Maybe it was simply his fate to achieve such amazing things in his life yet have no real happiness, only unrelenting misery.

Elvis wanted nothing more than to numb the pain he felt. And he knew exactly how to do it. He'd been doing it more or less for the last twenty years of his life. He got up and went to his bed. He moved the mattress aside and found the package of Demerol he'd hidden there.

Elvis wasn't completely sure what had made him buy them. Habit mostly. He hated the sleepless nights when they came and wanted to have a way to handle them if need be. Demerol would do the trick.

The night before heading to Vegas for his return concert, Elvis couldn't sleep at all. He'd been tempted then to take a couple pills, but had managed not to touch them. He'd worked so hard to detox, he didn't want to blow it. However, that wasn't the real reason he hadn't touched them. He didn't want to disappoint Vicky Lynn by going back to them.

Still, he'd kept them. He liked knowing the pills were there in case he ever needed them. He'd begun to hope he wouldn't. But the way his life had been turned completely upside down in the last twenty-four hours, it relieved him to know he had the Demerol.

Elvis pulled the bottle of pills from its hiding place. He stepped into the bathroom and filled a glass from the faucet. He dropped two Demerol pills into his palm and tossed them into his mouth. Elvis raised the water glass to wash them down his throat, where they'd wash his internal misery away as they had so many times before.

Before he could take a drink, his eyes landed on the pictures of Lisa Marie and her children that he'd found with the Google machine and from the computer. He'd taped them to the bathroom mirror to keep him motivated as he got his life together. The pictures were to remind him of why he was doing all he was doing to get sober and into good health.

Elvis gave his full attention to the picture of his adult daughter. Lisa Marie had truly grown into a beautiful woman during the years he'd been gone. His thoughts circled around all the years he'd missed with her. He could feel all the pain his early death had likely caused her. He had so many regrets. He'd been an addict and denied it.

It had cost him everything.

His family. His life. Everything.

And there he stood, doing it all over yet again. He didn't know any better. It was what he did.

He should've listened to Jackie Gleason and never given up being a regular guy. He should've stayed with Sam Phillips and not gone with Colonel Parker. Mr. Phillips had always been good to him. He'd really cared about Elvis and his career. It was why he'd sold Elvis's contract to RCA. Sam knew they could get Elvis national exposure when Sun Records couldn't.

Would it have mattered in the end? If he'd stayed with Sam and the Sun label, maybe he wouldn't have been as big, but he would've lived a normal life. If he had lived a normal life, then he probably wouldn't have been such a failure as a husband, as a father, and as a son.

Yes. He'd failed as a son. He'd failed his mother. Sure, he'd become the biggest singer of all time, but he'd lost so much that had been important to him.

Mama had always worried about his soul. When she was alive, she'd sounded off when things didn't feel right to her. She never trusted the Colonel. Elvis should've listened to her instincts. That was what he should've done. He'd probably have married Dixie Locke, like Mama had wanted. Dixie would have made a good wife. They would've had a few kids. Today, they'd have plenty of grandkids running around.

But that hadn't happened. He went for the fame and fortune, and it had destroyed him. Now it was about to do it again. Elvis knew his mother would be ashamed if she could see him now.

Maybe she could. Maybe she was looking down from heaven watching him right then. What would his mama say to him if she could talk to him right now?

The thought made Elvis pause. He could see her face in his mind's eye. He could hear Mama speaking to him.

Elvis, you was spared for a reason. That's why you lived instead of

Jesse. And that's why you got cloned. You've got a second chance for a reason.

Elvis shook his head, hoping to clear it.

What was that?

Had that been some sort of a hallucination? Did his mother really speak to him right then? Was it all part of his imagination?

Elvis wasn't sure, but one thing became crystal clear to him. Whether her voice was real or not, she was right. Mama always was. She'd always looked out for him and said what no one else would, regardless of what they thought.

He spat the two pills into the sink then poured the water out of the glass on top of them. The pills swirled down the drain.

Elvis wasn't going to throw in the towel. He'd never been a quitter. True, at times he'd been complacent and enjoyed the ride, but he'd never been a quitter. He wasn't quitting now.

He wasn't going to let Cameron Ogilvie get away with his scheme, either. Nobody owned Elvis Presley. Not this time. He was his own man, even if he might be a clone.

Elvis had a plan. It was crazy, but they'd always called Elvis crazy. And this plan was crazy enough to work. If it still could work.

Elvis pushed the thought out of his mind. One way or the other, it would work. It had to. He'd make it work.

He returned to the bedroom and reached under the mattress. He grabbed the rest of the pills and also pulled out the prepaid mobile phone he'd bought. The "burner" had arrived with the pills and the jewelry. He'd kept it hidden in case he ever needed it in an emergency. His current situation clearly qualified as such.

Elvis had programmed Victoria's number into his burner. He powered it up and dialed her up.

Victoria answered on the third ring. He could tell she didn't know who was calling.

"How you doing, Vicky Lynn?" he said.

"Elvis?" she asked.

"The one and only."

"You know I'm not supposed to be talking to you."

"I do, but I need your help."

"Your best bet is to let Mitchi file the appeal. She'll probably have a better chance at the Ninth Circuit than she did with Rentz today."

"To heck with the courts. Like that song I sing says, I'm doing it my way. But I can't do it without you."

Victoria didn't reply. Elvis could tell she was mulling things over. She was in deep water with Cameron. How much further would she want to go, especially if it risked her going to jail?

Finally, she said, "Okay. What do you need me to do?"

"Get in touch with an old friend of mine named Hank Miceli. He's over in Santa Monica. I don't have a phone number for him, but I do got an address. I need you to go see him tonight—"

"Tonight?"

"Yeah, tonight. Cameron wants to leave for New York in the morning, so I've got to be gone before then."

"All right," Victoria said. "What's his address?"

Elvis read it to her from the pad where he'd written it down months ago.

"Go see him right now," Elvis said. "And take him this message for me."

CHAPTER 49

HANK MICELI WAS ENJOYING THE second round of *Jeopardy!* when someone knocked on his door. *What the hell? Who comes around during Jeopardy!?*

Miceli got up from his recliner and felt his way to the door.

He opened it and said to the unexpected visitor he could not see, "Someone better have died and left me a million dollars if you're disturbing me during the middle of Double Jeopardy."

"Are you Hank Miceli?" a woman asked him.

"You wouldn't be here if I wasn't, so who's standing at my door?"

"My name's Victoria Hadley," she said.

Hank's face tightened. "I know who you are. You're the broad who claims she cloned Elvis."

"I don't appreciate the label, but yes, I did clone Elvis."

"Then you won't want to stick around for any other labels I might have for you."

Hank shut his door on her.

"I have a message for you," Victoria said through the door. "J.B.'s got the sniffles."

Hank froze as he heard the words. How did she know that phrase? She couldn't. Could she?

He reopened the door.

"What the hell did you just say?" he asked.

"J.B.'s got the sniffles," Victoria repeated.

"How do you know to tell me that?"

"Because Elvis told me to come here and say it to you."

Hank couldn't believe his ears. "It really is him…"

"Yes. I know this has been a shock to everyone."

"Lady, you don't know the half of it. Where is he?"

"Brentwood. I know this is going to sound crazy, but he asked me to come get you and take you to Santa Monica Airport."

"If it wasn't crazy, it wouldn't be Elvis," Hank said, and walked over to his recliner. "Come in here and help me find my coat. I also need to make a phone call."

Hank knew exactly where the phone was on the table beside his chair. He picked up the receiver. He used the braille on the phone's buttons to dial a number he knew by heart. Charlene answered on the second ring.

"Hey there, you sober?" Hank asked. "Good. You're not going to believe the charter we've got tonight."

CHAPTER 50

ELVIS WAITED UNTIL MIDNIGHT TO make his move. Cameron typically went to bed around ten thirty. Elvis was pretty sure that by this time he'd be able to get off the property without anyone noticing. He'd instructed Victoria to get Hank and meet him down the street at midnight.

Elvis approached the front gate. He'd found the combination on Cameron's computer and punched in the numbers on the keypad. The motors whirled and the gate slid open.

He was going to make it. Then the security lights popped on. Elvis turned to find Cameron approaching with Fatu a few steps behind him.

"I suggest you get back in the guesthouse," Cameron said. "You've got a busy day and a long tour ahead of you starting tomorrow."

"I ain't nobody's property," Elvis said. "Wasn't the Colonel's, and I ain't yours."

"Go back in there, now," Cameron said.

Elvis broke into a fighting stance. "You're gonna have to make me."

Elvis expected Cameron to signal Fatu forward to enforce his order. Elvis knew Fatu would be a real contest. He'd never beaten him. It would take all of his skill and strength for him to defeat the Samoan. But Cameron didn't send Fatu after him. Instead, he reached behind him and pulled a .45

that he pointed at Elvis's chest.

"Get back in the guesthouse, or I'm going to blow your ignorant redneck brains out the back of your skull."

Cameron was cold enough to shoot him. Elvis knew this. He also knew he wouldn't.

"You'd never pull the trigger," Elvis said. "I'm worth too much money to you."

Cameron smiled. "If studying everything about your life has taught me one thing, it's that you sell far more music when you're dead than when you're alive and swiveling."

Elvis felt his heart skip a beat. He'd underestimated Cameron.

"I'm done playing games with you," Cameron said, not lowering his pistol. "You're going on this tour and you're going to perform your ass off. Anything less, and your obsessed fans will have a second gravesite where they can come and pay their respects to you."

"So you're willing to murder me for the money?" Elvis asked.

"Weren't you listening in court?" Cameron said. "The law doesn't consider you a human being. Killing you wouldn't even be considered murder."

Elvis was stuck. Cameron was ruthless, even more so than the Colonel had been. Elvis had no doubt Cameron really would kill him and get away with it. He didn't see a way out of this now.

But if he could get Cameron close enough, he could probably disarm him. Elvis relaxed from his fighting stance and raised his hands over his head.

"All right," Elvis said. "You win."

"I always do," Cameron said. "Go earn your pay, fathead, and put the clone to bed."

Fatu took a step forward. Then, with an amazingly fast movement, he brought his fist up to Cameron's face. The blow smashed Cameron's nose. The balding music producer collapsed to the concrete.

Elvis couldn't believe it.

"Thanks," Elvis said. "Can't say I saw that coming."

Fatu shrugged. "He's an asshole."

"He made the Colonel seem like a saint."

Fatu gestured toward the front gate with his head. "Go," he told Elvis.

Elvis wondered what Fatu would do now. Maybe he could leave with him. There should be room on the plane. But before Elvis could ask anything, there was another voice in the dark.

"You're not going anywhere."

No. It wasn't another voice. It was Elvis's voice.

Elvis and Fatu turned as a man dressed in black stepped into the light. It wasn't merely a man. It was another Elvis.

How could that be? Had Victoria made another clone?

"Holy macaroni," Elvis said. "I thought there was only one clone of me."

"You mean there was," the man said. "You're about to become extinct."

The man pulled a pair of nunchucks from behind his back and swung them around his head and body in an expert fashion.

CHAPTER 51

MICHAEL PRESCOTT MOVED IN ON the clone and the big Samoan. He swung the nunchucks around his head, ready to strike.

"You get him from the left and I'll get him from the right," the clone told the Samoan.

Michael maneuvered and forced the clone to take a few steps back. Then Michael brought his attention to the Samoan. The Samoan leaped at him, but Michael had more speed. He stepped out of the way. With a series of kicks and blows from the nunchucks, he took the big Samoan down and knocked him out.

The clone of Elvis stared at Michael with absolute disbelief. Michael swung the nunchucks slowly as he circled the clone.

"You think you're pretty good with those, huh?" the clone said.

"No," Michael said. "I'm great with them."

"Well, I'm going to warn you. I'm an eighth-degree san black belt, trained by the great Master Kang Rhee himself."

"I know." Michael smiled then charged the clone.

Michael swung the nunchucks hard. The blows knocked the clone to the ground. Michael pressed the attack. The clone rolled out of the way. He really did have Elvis's fighting skills. The clone moved swiftly, and swept Michael's leg out from under him. Michael fell down on his back.

Both the clone and Michael got up at the same time. The two combatants warily circled each other.

"I don't know who trained you," Elvis's clone said. "But you're good."

"I studied you for years. I know everything about you, even all of your fighting styles. You can't beat me."

The clone threw a series of punches. Michael deflected them all.

"Man, who are you?" the clone asked.

"Isn't that sad?" Michael said. "I've idolized you every day of my life and you couldn't give a damn about me. You don't even care that you destroyed my life, do you?"

"Destroyed your life? Man, I don't even know who the heck you are."

Michael attacked with the nunchucks again. The clone caught one end of them. Each man held one end of the nunchucks, a brutal tug of war ensuing. They kicked and punched at each other. The fight was a stalemate for a long time, but then Michael landed a blow that dropped the clone to his knees.

The clone let go of the nunchuck. Michael grabbed it and pulled the bar around the clone's throat. Michael started choking him out. The clone struggled against him, but it didn't matter. Michael had the advantage. He pulled the wooden stick deeper against the clone's throat.

The clone was turning blue, the life draining out of him. This abomination, this twisted joke of science, would soon be dead.

CHAPTER 52

VICTORIA CHECKED THE CLOCK ON her phone for the third time within the minute. It was still 12:16 a.m., but Elvis had yet to show up at her car, where she waited with the blind Hank Miceli.

"You're worried," Hank said.

"He should be here by now," she said.

"Yeah. E was always Mr. Punctual."

"So's his clone."

Something had gone wrong. She couldn't prove it, but Victoria could feel it. Maybe Cameron had figured out Elvis was up to something. Or maybe he couldn't get off the property. She couldn't sit here and wait much longer. Someone would notice she and Hank parked here and call the police. She had to take a look.

Victoria opened the door and said, "Stay here. I'm going to go take a look."

"Not like I'm in the shape to take off on a joy ride anymore," Hank said.

Victoria closed the door and hurried down the street to Cameron's mansion. When she neared the gate, she could see the gate was opened and the security lights were on. Nearing the open gate, she saw Elvis on the ground being strangled by…Elvis?

What in the hell was going on?

No, Elvis wasn't being strangled by Elvis. It was a man

who looked remarkably like Elvis holding a pipe or something hard against Elvis's windpipe. Elvis couldn't even lift his arms to fight the man off. Elvis was being murdered by some deranged impersonator!

"Stop it!" she yelled. "You're killing him!"

The impersonator looked up. He was shocked to see her. Victoria rushed forward, and he responded by pulling the bar tighter against Elvis's throat.

"Stay away!" Michael yelled. "He's already dead."

Victoria stopped her advance. She wasn't sure if Elvis's heart had stopped yet. If it hadn't, the lack of oxygen would stop it soon enough. She had to do something, and fast, to have any hope of saving Elvis.

Victoria noticed Fatu and Cameron lying unconscious on the concrete nearby. Had Elvis done that as he tried to escape? Or were they victims of this insane impersonator?

Beside Cameron's right hand, Victoria noticed a gun. She ran over to it and picked it up. She'd never held a gun before. Her hand shook as she lifted it. She put her finger on the trigger and pointed it at the impersonator's head.

"Let him go," she said.

If the sight of her aiming the gun at his face scared him, the impersonator didn't let it show. He gritted his teeth and continued to press the bar against Elvis's neck.

Victoria cocked the pistol and took three steps forward. She put a second hand on the gun to steady herself. She had a clear shot at the impersonator's forehead.

"I'm not going to let you kill him," Victoria said.

The impersonator must have realized she was serious, even if Victoria wondered whether she could actually pull the trigger or not. He released Elvis.

The clone fell forward. They both looked at him. A second later, Elvis gasped for air. He was alive.

"Move away from him," Victoria told the impersonator,

not lowering the gun.

The man backed away, but still held the weapon he'd been using to choke Elvis.

"Drop those sticks," she said. The impersonator threw the chained bars away. They clanged against the concrete of the driveway.

Elvis climbed to his knees, then to his feet with some difficulty. The color was returning to his face. He rubbed his throat with one hand.

"Are you all right?" Victoria asked.

"Yeah," Elvis answered with a raspy voice. "Thanks to you."

Elvis turned his attention to the impersonator Victoria continued to hold at gunpoint.

"Man, who are you?" he asked the man.

"You don't even know," the impersonator cried out with great anguish. "You don't even know. You don't even know!"

But now that Elvis was safe and she was calming down, Victoria recognized him.

"I know who you are," she said. "You're one of the impersonators from the Elvis show at the Oasis."

"Tribute artist!" the impersonator yelled. "And I wasn't just one. I was the best in the world." He pointed at Elvis. "But then you cloned him and ruined everything for me."

Elvis took a few cautious steps toward the man. "I'm sorry," Elvis said. "But Vicky Lynn didn't mean to hurt nobody. Neither did I."

"Oh, you couldn't care less about me," the impersonator said. "You don't even know who the heck I am."

"No, I don't," Elvis said. "But since I've been back, I've learned what fellas like you were doing. You were taking care of the fans while I was, well, while I was out of the picture. I wouldn't have had any fans to come back to if it wasn't for all that y'all did for me."

Victoria noticed something changed with the impersonator. Elvis's words had touched him. The anger and the pain in the man's face melted away. Now he looked at Elvis with awe and appreciation, like she'd witnessed every fan do since his return.

"My mom always said you had the kindest eyes," the impersonator told Elvis.

Those words shocked Elvis and Victoria. She knew there had been paternity suits against Elvis before, but she wasn't aware that any claims made had ever been proven legitimate. Could this impersonator be Elvis's son?

Elvis must've been wondering the same thing. He asked the impersonator, "You saying I knew your mama? Wait, you're not…?"

"You met her once," the man said. "Back in the summer of '77. She brought your dinner up to your hotel room in Springfield, Missouri after you'd checked in."

Elvis paused and thought. "You mean Jennie who spells it with an IE?" Elvis asked.

His question astonished the impersonator. "You remember her?"

"Yeah," Elvis said. "I gave her an autograph before she left. Very sweet lady."

"She still is. It's framed and hanging in her living room. She always told me what an incredible man you were. You're all I ever wanted to be. And being that I was born the same day you died, I figured it was a sign it was meant to be."

"You were born on August sixteenth?" Elvis asked.

"August 16, 1977. I thought it was my reason for being here. But now that you're here, it's all gone now."

Cameron groaned and stirred on the ground nearby.

"Elvis," Victoria said, "if we're going to go, we should do it now."

Elvis looked to her and pointed to the impersonator with

his thumb. "You say he's pretty good at being me?"

"The only one better is you," she said.

"Think Cameron would notice the difference?" Elvis asked.

"What are you saying?" she asked.

"Exactly what you think I am."

"That's crazy," she said.

"Then it could work," Elvis said.

The impersonator said, "I feel like I'm missing something here."

Elvis turned to him. "You said you wanted to be me. How'd you like to get the chance?"

"You can't be serious," the impersonator said, but Victoria could see the hope in the man's eyes.

"As that heart attack I'm trying not to have," said Elvis. "But if you want to do it, there's one thing I'm going to need you to do."

CHAPTER 53

ELVIS CLIMBED INTO THE BACKSEAT of Victoria's Audi as she got behind the wheel. He wore Michael's clothes now. They'd switched their attire as Elvis explained what Michael needed to do if he wanted to take his place.

Elvis smiled as he saw his old friend Hank Miceli sitting in front of him in the passenger seat.

"Good to see you, Henri," Elvis said.

Elvis always enjoyed calling him by his name in French. He'd learned that during the one weekend he'd taken leave to go to Paris back in 1959.

"E, is it really you?" Hank asked, and turned around in the seat.

It had been forty years since Elvis had seen him. Hank's hair was thinner and white, his face lined with wrinkles and age, and the sight had gone from his eyes. But it was still him.

"No, it's Fats Domino," Elvis said.

Victoria started the car and headed off into the night as the two friends got reacquainted.

Hank reached up and felt Elvis's face, sideburns, and hair.

"It really is you!" Hank said, his disbelief apparent. "They really did clone you."

"Not they," Elvis said. "She. Is everything set?"

"Just as you wanted," Hank said. "But I'm not going to be able to fly you."

"Yeah, so it seems," Elvis said as he looked into Hank's sightless eyes. He clasped his friend's hand. "I'm sorry, Henri."

"Nothing to be sorry about," Hank said. "Things fall apart for all of us if we get a chance to live long enough."

"Well, that's what I'm trying to find out."

"I can't take the stick anymore, but my granddaughter, Charlene, can. She'll be doing the flying."

"She as good a pilot as you?" Elvis asked.

"She might even be better."

"Then I'll guess we'll be all right."

Elvis settled back into his seat. As happy as he was to see Hank and to have escaped, he was nervous. He'd gotten away from Cameron, but had he gotten away completely? That would all depend on how good Michael Prescott could impersonate him when the music producer came to.

CHAPTER 54

FATU HELPED CAMERON GET TO his feet as the producer regained consciousness. At the same time, Fatu held Michael at gunpoint.

Elvis had quickly brought Fatu up to speed on the plan, as the clone and Michael switched clothes. This was the moment of truth. Everything hinged on this. Cameron had to believe Michael was the clone. If he didn't, then they were all ruined.

"What the hell happened to me?" Cameron asked, wiping blood from his face.

"He attacked you," Fatu said. He gestured toward Michael with the pistol.

Cameron was confused. "*He* attacked me?"

Michael knew the moment had arrived. It was now or never. Channeling Elvis, he said to Cameron, "I'm an eighth-degree san black belt, trained by the great Master Kang Rhee. And I'm fast." He threw a flurry of punches, demonstrating his speed, then pointed to the gun at Fatu's hand. "Just not faster than a bullet."

"No, you're not," Cameron said.

Michael relaxed. Cameron was falling for it.

"Good work, Fatu," Cameron said, then took the gun from his bodyguard. He pointed it at Michael. The producer had an intense look on his face. It frightened Michael.

"Whoa," Michael said, raising his hands over his head.

"Wait a minute, Mr. Ogilvie—"

"Wait for what?" Cameron said. "For you to assault me again, Mr. Karate? I don't think so."

What had that damn clone gotten him into? Michael needed to think fast or he'd be dead before living a single day as Elvis.

"Let's be reasonable," Michael said.

"I don't believe you can be," Cameron said.

"Look, Mr. Ogilvie," Michael said, "you know I don't like this arrangement with you—"

"I could care less what you like or you don't."

"I'll do the tour," Michael blurted out. "And anything else you want."

"You've got that damn right."

"But I've got one condition."

"Why isn't it clear to you that the days of you putting on conditions are long since over?" Cameron asked.

"I know that. I don't like it, but I know it. All I'm asking for is one thing. If you'll do that, you won't have any more hassles out of me."

"Oh, really?" Cameron said with suspicion. "After all you've put me through, you're willing to wave the white flag that easily?"

"I really don't have much of a choice," Michael said. He then kept his word that he'd given the clone as part of their bargain. "All I'm asking is that you stand by your word to Dr. Hadley."

"What goes on between me and Victoria is none of your damn business."

"You and I know if it weren't for her, I wouldn't be here," Michael said. "And I know you're steamed at her for a lot of reasons. But you're going to make a ton of money because of me. The least you can do is give her what you promised her for her research."

"You care for her that much, do you?" Cameron asked.

"Yeah. I do."

Michael watched as Cameron weighed it all over while keeping the gun pointed at him.

"I'll never drop the restraining order," Cameron said. "Your days with my ex are over."

"I understand that," Michael said. "I just want you to do right by her."

Cameron finally lowered his gun.

"All right," Cameron said. "You bring your A-game to *Saturday Night Live* this weekend and I'll wire her the appropriate funds."

It had worked! Cameron believed Michael was Elvis and had agreed to his one term.

"Thank you, Mr. Ogilvie," Michael said, smiling. "I really do appreciate it."

"But if this is some ploy of yours or I find out that you're trying to con me," Cameron said, holding the gun up, "then it's a-dios, Elvis."

"Mr. Ogilvie, I know better than to try to con a man like you."

CHAPTER 55

VICTORIA DROVE DIRECTLY TO THE hangar Hank had instructed her to go to.

As she, Elvis, and Hank exited the car, a woman of about thirty emerged from the hangar. Hank introduced her to them as Charlene.

Like so many others, Charlene was awestruck by meeting Elvis.

"It's incredible to meet you," she said. "Grandpa's told me so many stories about you."

"Hopefully not too many," Elvis said. "Some of our stories weren't quite fit for ladies' ears."

Hank laughed. "Don't worry about her. She's like one of the boys. And she knows exactly what needs to be done to cure J.B.'s sniffles."

"Sounds good to me," Elvis said. "How many passengers can you take?"

"One plus you," Charlene answered.

Elvis turned to Victoria. "That seat's for you if you want it," he told her.

"I know," Victoria said. "But you also know I can't go with you."

"I do. Just like me, you're here for a purpose too."

They stared at each other. Elvis didn't want to leave her, even though he knew he had to.

"There's no guarantee he'll give me the funds," Victoria

said.

"I think he'll know a good deal when he hears it," Elvis said.

"Maybe," Victoria said. "On top of being greedy, Cameron can be remarkably stubborn, as you've seen."

"Well, if he doesn't come through, you can always find Hank or Charlene. They'll know how to get you to me."

"I know," she said. "But even if he doesn't send the money, I'll have to go back out there to raise it on my own. You know I have to keep moving forward with my work."

"That I do. But if I didn't ask you to come with me, I'd never forgive myself."

Elvis took her in under the light from the hangar. Vicky Lynn was the most amazing woman he'd ever met in his entire life. He hated that he might never see her again.

"I ain't ever been too good at goodbyes," he said.

"Me either," she said. "I'll never forget you."

"Well, I am kinda unforgettable," Elvis said with a grin.

"And always so full of humility."

"That's how my mama raised me."

Elvis gently touched her cheek with two fingers. Her skin was so soft.

"It's because of you that I'm here," he said. "You saved me, Vicky Lynn. And more than once, as things turned out."

"And if things work out, you may have saved my son."

Victoria moved closer and kissed Elvis. It was the kind of deep, passionate kiss that lasted a lifetime in one's memories. Or, at least, Elvis would always remember it that way.

CHAPTER 56

SEVEN HOURS, THREE TIME ZONES, and over three thousand miles from Los Angeles, Elvis stood with Hank and Charlene on a tropical beach, watching the sun set into the endless Pacific Ocean. Charlene had flown them to this small island west of Hawaii. Except for its native population, the place was deserted and had escaped the progress of time. It was a place where life could be reinvented and made new.

"How did you find out about this island?" Charlene asked.

"We came over on weekends while he was filming *Paradise, Hawaiian Style*," Hank said.

"No," Elvis said. "It was during *Girls! Girls! Girls!*"

"That's right," Hank said. "I get your Hawaii movies mixed up."

"*Blue Hawaii* was the only one worth a damn," Elvis said. "Anyway, your granddaddy brought me over here so I could get away when things got to be a little too much. I figured if I ever quit to get away from it all, I'd come here. But I didn't get a chance to do that before."

"Don't be so sure about that," Hank said.

Elvis looked at Hank. "What are you saying, Henri?"

Before Hank could answer, Elvis heard a familiar voice.

"I was starting to wonder if you'd turn up here."

Elvis spun around. An old man with thick white hair and sideburns, using a bamboo cane to walk, approached them.

He had a Polynesian woman in her forties on his arm.

Elvis looked at the old man. The old man stared back at him. They stood looking each other in the eyes. Their eyes were completely identical.

The clone knew exactly who this man was it. It was him. It was Elvis!

"Holy macaroni," the clone said.

"You can say that again," the older Elvis said.

"Guess I did fake my own death," the clone said.

"You got no memory of planning it?" Elvis asked.

"Yeah, but I didn't know how I was going to pull it off. Everything with Lisa Marie and everyone else. You know, I think it affected her really bad."

The eighty-three-year-old Elvis lowered his eyes. "And I regret that more than you can imagine," he said. "But things were getting so out of control, if I didn't do it then, I'd wind up dead. Ain't that right, Henri?"

"You were in pretty bad shape when I first got you out here, E," Hank said. He stepped forward and felt the older Elvis's face.

"Didn't think I'd ever be seeing you again either," Elvis said.

"I didn't think I'd be helping you escape your life again," Hank said.

This was still a lot for the clone to take in.

"You've been living here the whole time?" he asked.

"It's been a good place to hide," Elvis said.

"I'll say so," the clone said.

"You both did," Hank said.

Elvis stepped over to his clone. "I saw what that dang Ogilvie was doing to you. I was wondering if you'd remember about this island and come here."

"Think I could ever forget this place?"

"Neither of us could. Welcome to paradise."

Elvis opened his arms up. The clone came forward and hugged the original.

"Why don't we head on over to the house?" the older Elvis said to everyone. "We're about the spit a pig, so there's more than enough for everybody."

"Hold the horses," the clone said. "How old are you?"

"Turned eighty-three in January."

"And you didn't have no heart attacks?"

"Once I dropped the weight and got off them pills, my ticker's been doing fine."

"Well hot damn," the clone said. "You think maybe we could fry up a peanut butter and banana sandwich? I ain't had one in forever."

"Of course. And we fry 'em in real bacon fat."

The clone smiled. "Just like Mama did."

"That's why Mama's were always the best," Elvis said.

CHAPTER 57

THE STILL-UNEMPLOYED TY VANDEKAMP SAT alone in his apartment and turned his TV to NBC. The clone of Elvis was hosting *Saturday Night Live* that evening.

As he'd been in concert, the clone was amazing. He sang four songs and performed in nearly every skit. His comedic timing was perfect. Elvis, as he'd always been, was a natural entertainer. No doubt Hollywood would be calling soon. Hopefully, Elvis would be more discriminating in picking his projects this time around.

Ty's phone chimed. It was Eddie Zee. Eddie had wrapped up two shows that night in his new gig as David Bowie. Eddie was hungry and wanted to see if Ty wanted to grab a bite. Ty agreed to meet him over at Hash House A Go Go. That was where he, Eddie, and Michael often went after wrapping up their *One Night with Elvis* shows at the Oasis.

Ty wondered about Michael. He hadn't been seen or heard from in days. His phone no longer went to voice mail when Ty called to check on him. Nothing happened, as if the number had been completely disconnected.

Ty hoped Michael was all right, wherever he had run off to.

CHAPTER 58

THE AFTER-PARTY FOR *Saturday Night Live* was incredible. *SNL* cast members, current and former, had all come to see Michael Prescott. Well, not him, Michael needed to remind himself, but Elvis Presley.

Even Eddie Murphy, who had been a huge Elvis fan, had attended the taping to meet Elvis after. Eddie and Elvis took a photo that Cameron put out on Twitter. In less than an hour, it was one of the most retweeted images ever. And if the social media buzz was any indicator, this episode of *SNL* would be the highest rated of the season, if not of the show's entire history.

Michael noticed that both Cameron and Fatu kept a very close eye on him at the after-party. As the party wound down and drunken attendees stumbled their way out the door, Michael took a seat across from Cameron.

"Well, what do you think, Mr. Ogilvie?"

"I think bringing you back remains the most genius idea I've ever had," Cameron said.

"I didn't just bring the A-game tonight. I brought the A-plus-game."

"And you want to make sure I stick to our little side agreement."

"Yes, sir," Michael said.

"The money will start flowing to her on Monday morning," Cameron said, and leaned closer to the man he believed was his Elvis clone. "But if you're anything short of enthusiastic and mesmerizing at any point of this tour, you won't like what I do."

"You've got nothing to worry about, Mr. Ogilvie. The people want Elvis, and that's what I'm here to give them—Elvis."

CHAPTER 59

VICTORIA RECEIVED A PHONE CALL from Skylar Kauffman on Monday morning. Cameron Stone had agreed to wire twenty million dollars to Bio-Design to settle any and all claims she might have against his client from her work cloning Elvis Presley.

She couldn't believe it. Like the rest of the country, Victoria had watched *SNL* that weekend. If she hadn't known the truth, she would have believed he was Elvis. Michael Prescott really was the world's greatest tribute artist. He had to be to trick someone like Cameron Ogilvie.

Two days later, Victoria met with Skylar at CEO Music's offices to sign a confidential structured settlement for the duration of Elvis's tour. Victoria left his office and immediately started making phone calls. She needed to rehire all of the essential staff members she'd been forced to lay off when her money had dried up.

Most of them were available to come back to Bio-Design. They needed to give two-week notices, which was fine. One of her best scientists, however, had major reservations about accepting the offer to return.

"Dr. Hadley," she said, "I really don't want my talents merely used to bring back dead celebrities so that rich people like your ex-husband can become even richer. It goes against my principles and the very reasons I got into genetics in the first place."

"I understand completely," Victoria reassured her. "Given my recent experiences with human cloning, I'm not all that eager to continue down that path either. What I'd like to focus our efforts on is using our combined knowledge to cure hereditary diseases. Specifically, I'd like to put our minds to cracking the genetic code that will lead to the ability to repair and prevent Hunter syndrome."

CHAPTER 60

ON A MOSTLY DESERTED TROPICAL island west of Hawaii, an eighty-three-year-old Elvis Presley jammed with his forty-two-year-old clone.

The two Elvises played all of the old standards that had earned them stacks of gold records. They sang gospel hymns and reminisced about all of their friends and families who had passed on in the last four decades. The clone performed the new songs he'd learned for Elvis. They sang and played until the sun came up on their island. And they ate until they couldn't force another bite down their throats.

It was one of the best nights the clone had experienced in a long time. He looked over at his older self, the original whose DNA from forty years ago had brought him to life. He watched as the smiling, silver-haired man most people believed dead and buried in the Meditation Garden at Graceland played riffs on the guitar.

Nope, the clone thought.

Elvis wasn't dead. Elvis was still alive.

Long live the King of Rock and Roll.

Long live Elvis Presley.

HOW DID ELVIS DO IT?

Now that you've reached the end of *Cloning Elvis* you're probably asking yourself how exactly did Elvis manage to fake his own death in 1977?

How could the world's biggest and most recognizable star pull of such hoax?

Take a trip back in time and learn exactly how he did it in this FREE original short story prequel, *Saving Elvis*.

Get your FREE digital copy of Saving Elvis now at this link:
BrianDavidFloyd.com/SavingElvis
briandavidfloyd.com/savingelvis

ACKNOWLEDGEMENTS

No story is ever conceived or completed in a vacuum, especially this one. I must give my deepest thanks and appreciation to the following people:

Mike Prisco – If you hadn't infected me with the Elvis bug years ago, I'd have had no reason to tell this story.

Robert Hammond – You once told me a producer said he'd kill the next writer who pitched him the idea of "cloning Jesus." That got me thinking; if you can't clone the King of Kings, then why not clone the King of Rock and Roll?

Riley J. Ford – Your feedback helped improve this story and your enthusiasm for it pushed me to publish it.

Thaine Allison, Kim Adelman, and Stephanie Vanderham – Thank you for providing input on the rough draft that has helped make this story better.

Tony Wyman, Stacey Hoag, Jodie Myers, Pedro Pano, and Stephanie Vanderham – I appreciate your suggestions of songs for the clone of Elvis to sing here in 2018. All of those songs wound up included in the book.

As you might imagine, a significant amount of research went into writing this book. Here are the main points of research that informed and inspired me during the creative process:

Being Elvis: A Lonely Life by Ray Connolly is a terrific new biography of Elvis. I gleaned most of the details about Elvis and his life that I used in this book from Ray's stellar work.

Elvis in the Morning by William F. Buckley is not only an insightful and entertaining book, it also showed me how to properly put Elvis into a work of fiction as a character.

Bring Back the King: The New Science of De-extinction by Helen Pilcher demonstrated that the idea of cloning Elvis Presley isn't as crazy as it might seem, though it certainly wouldn't play out the way it does in my book.

Is Elvis Alive? by Gail Brewer-Giorgio and its accompanying cassette tape, which I first picked up back in 1988, definitely inspired the ending of this story.

I also visited Graceland and Sun Studio in Memphis, Tennessee last summer. Walking in those places where Elvis once did helped give me a real sense of him as a living, breathing person. Being around so many of his devoted fans from all over the world also made it clear that I couldn't rush this book if I wanted to do justice to Elvis. I hope I've succeeded.

Brian David Floyd
Pasadena, California
January 2018

ABOUT THE AUTHOR

Brian David Floyd is the author of *Livin' on a Prayer* (written with Robert Slawsby*)*, *Last Wishes*, *The Short Stack*, and the comically touching memoir *Dad Was Right: 10 Life Lessons a Father Taught His Son.*

When he's not reading, writing, or doing that work thing, Brian enjoys country dancing, exploring the United States and its history, impersonating Elvis Presley, and pretty much anything involving *Star Wars.*

Brian is a native of Southern California who has immigrated to Nashville, Tennessee. He is currently working on his next books.

You can learn more about Brian, what he's up to, and discover free original stories on his website:
BrianDavidFloyd.com

Made in the USA
Coppell, TX
20 August 2022

81764830R00132